Thomas Carlyle

**On the Choice of Books**

Thomas Carlyle

**On the Choice of Books**

ISBN/EAN: 9783337280796

Printed in Europe, USA, Canada, Australia, Japan

Cover: Foto ©Andreas Hilbeck / pixelio.de

More available books at **www.hansebooks.com**

ON THE

# *CHOICE OF BOOKS*

BY

THOMAS CARLYLE.

*FIFTH EDITION.*

WITH A NEW LIFE OF THE AUTHOR.

*No. 5, Great Cheyne Row, Chelsea,*
THE RESIDENCE OF MR. CARLYLE SINCE 1834.

𝕷𝖔𝖓𝖉𝖔𝖓:

CHATTO AND WINDUS, PUBLISHERS.
1878.

# PRELIMINARY.

THE general belief that Carlyle is a gloomy misanthrope, scarcely ever seen outside his own door, is quite an error. Like Thackeray—and, indeed, most other sensible authors—he has no disinclination to accept an invitation to a good dinner. Only a short time ago, he was the guest of the fashionable young officers on guard at St. James's Palace, who were delighted at having the great man amongst them—and in full talk, too. It was not like any ordinary conversation—says one that was present—it was as if the speaker was giving a long recitation from some favourite book—an essay, a philosophical poem thrown into prose—and experienced a tranquil, steady pleasure from the recital. He touched upon his best-beloved topics, and held forth their excellencies, as some ancient philosopher might have done when moving amongst his scholars in those early schools of the classic period, which have been imagined in the designs of the old masters. Carlyle's conversation is, perhaps, the best living representation of Coleridge's style and manner.

He has, however, a strong dislike to make himself conspicuous in any way. In his own neighbourhood of Chelsea he is never known to take part in public affairs, parochial or otherwise. He has, in short, a horror of the stump and the "Vestry Hall." The suburb, however, has evidently attractions for him of a peculiar kind. Leigh Hunt's removal to Chelsea was owing to him, as all readers of Hunt's correspondence will remember. Hunt lived in Upper Cheyne Row, within a stone's throw of his illustrious friend; and many were the visits between the two houses, Carlyle being always ready to step in when any of those little difficulties about the water-rate, or the butcher's bill, which "vex the poet's mind," required the prompt assistance of a friend, whose motto was *bis dat qui cito dat.* Retired as is Carlyle's life, his gaunt figure, attired in a brown coat, and dark horn buttons, and with a

large, slouched felt hat, is familiar enough to
Chelsea people. Nor will the denizens of that
historico-literary locality let him pass quite so
unnoticed as he would desire. Already a sort of
pre-posthumous fame has gathered about him;
and the gentlemen who wrote the life of Turner,
and collected so much about that immortal
genius from Chelsea folks, would find Chelsea
no less fruitful of anecdote about Carlyle. There
they tell how the great author of " Hero Worship" one day found himself without three-pence
to pay a fare, and how an irreverent omnibus
conductor, having evidently strong doubts of his
character, deputed a sharp newspaper boy to
accompany him to the .address he had given, and
see "all was right ;" and how the boy was in-
terrogated by the philosopher with " Weel, cawn
ye read ?" and so forth ; and found him " a very
nice man," and hastened to the omnibus conductor to communicate the fact, that the supposed
cheat was "a gentleman, and really did live in
Great Cheyne Row, as he had solemnly alleged."

Carlyle always walks at night, carrying an
enormous stick, and generally with his eyes on
the ground. When he is in London any one may
be sure of meeting him in some of the dark

streets of that locality about midnight, taking his constitutional walk before retiring to bed—a custom which he continued all through the "garrotting" panic, in spite of warnings of friends that the history of Frederick the Great might one day be brought to an untimely and premature conclusion. Probably the philosopher was quite willing to trust to his knotted stick, although walking alone, as is his invariable custom. Occasionally he may be seen on horseback; and the good Chelsea folks, whom the philosopher will doubtless pardon for a little excess of that form of "hero-worship" which delights in accumulating details about "living celebrities," tell how he grooms his own horse, keeping it in a stable on an odd piece of waste ground, among donkeys, cows, and geese, who have also their abodes there, and from the crazy gateway of which he issues forth, always unattended, sitting erect in the saddle, like a skeleton guardsman. His solitary habits, however, are not altogether unbroken. Though it is rare indeed that he is ever seen to stop and speak to a grown person in the street—probably because he knows but one or two personally in his own neighbourhood—he is always ready to recognise little children.  The keeper of a small confectioner's shop near the river-side tells with delight how he will call upon her for extravagant quantities of cheap sweetmeats, with which he will sometimes stop and load the laps of a little group of poor children in some of the purlieux of Lawrence Street—that locality once hallowed by the presence of Smollett, Toland, and Budgell—but now, alas ! sadly fallen from its old gentility.

Some popular anecdotes of him, however, are not, it must be confessed, of so genial a character.  Mr. Babbage himself is not more sensitive to street noises, for which reason—this was before the days of Mr. Bass's bill—our philosopher would often be seen to rush out without his hat to offer the proprietor of a dreadful organ a bribe ; failing which he would seize the outlandish offender by the coat collar and forcibly deposit him, instrument and all, at the door of a neighbouring literary man, who had rendered himself conspicuous by defending the organ-grinding nuisance in the public press.  Equally famous in that locality is his hatred of fowls and their noise: a neighbour's fowls having, as he once complained, succeeded in banishing him to an upper garret, because, as he said in his peculiar broad Doric, "they would neither hatch in peace nor let him." Generally, however, the philosopher and historian's friends may be glad to know that he enjoys a degree of retirement and seclusion not easily to be found in the suburbs of the metropolis. The street in which he resides is silent, deserted, and antique. A large garden, fit for philosophic meditation, and enclosed in fine old red brick walls—strangely neglected, by the way, and exhibiting all the "rank luxuriance" of the jungle—lies at the back of the house, where "rumours of the outward world" rarely reach him; and where, we hope, we may be pardoned for this brief, but not irreverent glance at the far-famed Philosopher of Chelsea.

JOHN CAMDEN HOTTEN.

# BIOGRAPHICAL · INTRODUCTION.

THERE comes a time in the career of every man of genius who has devoted a long life to the instruction and enlightenment of his fellow-creatures, when he receives before his death all the honours paid by posterity. Thus when a great essayist or historian lives to attain a classic and world-wide fame, his own biography becomes as interesting to the public as those he himself has written, and by which he achieved his laurels.

This is almost always the case when a man of such cosmopolitan celebrity outlives the ordinary allotted period of threescore years and ten; for a younger generation has then sprung up, who only hear of his great fame, and are ignorant of the long and painful steps by which it was achieved. These remarks are peculiarly applicable in regard to the man whose career we are now to dwell on for a short time : his genius was of slow growth and development, and his fame was even more tardy in coming ; but since the world some thirty years ago fairly recognised him as a great and original thinker and teacher, few men have left so indelible an impress on the public mind, or have influenced to so great a degree the most thoughtful minds of the time.

Thomas Carlyle was born on Tuesday, December 4th, 1795, near Ecclefechan, a small village in the district of Annandale, Dumfriesshire. His father, an agriculturist, was noted for quickness of mental perception, and great energy and decision of character; his mother, as affectionate, pious, and more than ordinarily intelligent ;* and thus accepting his own

---

* "Carlyle's mother was a person, it seems, who had through her spiritual instincts discovered that the ordinary views (the received version, in fact) regarding the character of Cromwell were incorrect. She was, apparently, very much such a person as the female head of the household delineated in the ' Cotter's Saturday Night.' It was through his mother that Carlyle was led to undertake the labour of clearing up the character of this British worthy."

theory, that "the history of a man's childhood is the description of his parents' environment," Carlyle entered upon the "mystery of life" under happy and enviable circumstances.   After preliminary instruction, first at the parish school, and afterwards at Annan, he went, in November, 1809, and when he was fourteen years old, to the University of Edinburgh.   Here he remained for seven or eight years, distinguishing himself by his devotion to mathematical studies then taught there by Professor Leslie.   As a student, he was irregular in his application, but when he did set to work, it was with his whole energy.   He appears to have been a great reader of general literature at this time, and the stories that are told of the books that he got through are scarcely to be credited.   It was at school that Carlyle formed a friendship with Edward Irving, with whom he maintained an intercourse during the whole time of his attendance at the University.   Although Carlyle had, at his parents' desire, commenced his studies with a view to entering the Scottish Church, the idea of becoming a minister was abandoned long before he left college.   A fellow-student describes his habits at this time as lonely and contemplative ; and we know from another source that his vacations were principally spent among the hills and by the rivers of his native county. When he left Edinburgh he seems to have been completely undecided as to his future course. However, two vacancies occurring just at this time in schools at Dysart, in Fifeshire, and in Kirkcaldy, he, and his friend Irving, engaged themselves as teachers, Carlyle taking the post of tutor in mathematics, as he had distinguished himself in that branch at the university. He remained here about two years, becoming more and more convinced that neither as minister nor as schoolmaster was he to successfully fight his way up in the world. It had become clear to him that literature was his true vocation, and he would have started in the profession at once had it been convenient for him to do so.

He had already written several articles and essays, and a few of them had appeared in print; but they gave little promise or indication of the power he was afterwards to exhibit. During the years 1820—1823, he contributed a series of articles (biographical and topographical) to Brewster's " Edinburgh Encyclopædia,"* viz. :—

* Vols. XIV. to XVI. The fourteenth volume bears at the

1. Lady Mary Wortley Montagu
2. Montaigne
3. Montesquieu
4. Montfaucon
5. Dr. Moore
6. Sir John Moore
7. Necker
8. Nelson
9. Netherlands
10. Newfoundland
11. Norfolk
12. Northamptonshire
13. Northumberland
14. Mungo Park
15. Lord Chatham
16. William Pitt.

The following is from the article on *Necker* :—

" As an author, Necker displays much irregular force of imagination, united with considerable perspicuity and compass of thought ; though his speculations are deformed by an undue attachment to certain leading ideas, which, harmonizing with his habits of mind, had acquired an excessive preponderance in the course of his long and uncontroverted meditations. He possessed extensive knowledge, and his works bespeak a philosophical spirit ; but their great and characteristic

---

end the imprint, "Edinburgh, printed by Balfour and Clarke, 1820 ;" and the sixteenth volume, " Printed by A. Balfour and Co., Edinburgh, 1823." Most of these articles are distinguished by the initials " T. C." ; but they are all attributed to Carlyle in the List of the Authors of the Principal Articles, prefixed to the work on its completion.

excellence proceeds from that glow of fresh and youthful admiration for everything that is amiable or august in the character of man, which, in Necker's heart, survived all the blighting vicissitudes it had passed through, *combining, in a singular union, the fervour of the stripling with the experience of the sage.*"*

Here is a passage from the article on *Newfoundland*, interesting as containing perhaps the earliest germ of the later style :—

" The ships intended for the fishery on the southeast coast, arrive early in June. Each takes her station opposite any unoccupied part of the beach where the fish may be most conveniently cured, and retains it till the end of the season. Formerly the master who arrived first on any station was constituted *fishing-admiral*, and had by law the power of settling disputes among the other crews. But the jurisdiction

---

* When this article was written, Carlyle's mind must already have been thoroughly imbued with the poetry of Schiller, whose Life he was shortly to publish. The words printed in italics are an almost literal translation of the concluding lines of Schiller's poem, entitled *Licht und Wärme :*—

" Drum paart zu eurem schönsten Glück
  Mit Schwärmers Ernst des Weltmanns Blick !"

of those *admirals* is now happily superseded by the regular functionaries who reside on shore. Each captain directs his whole attention to the collection of his own cargo, without minding the concerns of his neighbour. Having taken down what part of the rigging is removable, they set about their laborious calling, and must pursue it zealously. Their mode of proceeding is thus described by Mr. Anspach, *a clerical person, who lived in the island several years, and has since written a meagre and very confused book, which he calls a* HISTORY *of it."*

To the "New Edinburgh Review" (1821-22) Carlyle also contributed two papers—one on Joanna Baillie's "Metrical Legends," and one on Goethe's "Faust."

In the year 1822 he made a translation of "Legendre's Geometry," to which he prefixed an Essay on Proportion; and the book appeared a year or two afterwards under the auspices of the late Sir David Brewster.* The Essay on Proportion remains to

---

* "Elements of Geometry and Trigonometry," with Notes. Translated from the French of A. M. Legendre. Edited by David Brewster, LL.D. With Notes and Additions, and an Introductory Chapter on Proportion. Edinburgh: published

this day the most lucid and succinct exposition of the subject hitherto published.

During some portion of this unsettled period of his life, Carlyle took up his residence in Germany, where he remained for a considerable length of time. It was there that he not only acquired that accurate knowledge of the German language, and that intimate acquaintance with German literature, which has since excited in so large a degree the admiration of scholars, but that he formed a friendly and familiar intimacy with Goethe. So great was the friendship which the latter entertained for him, and so fond was he of his society, that, as he could not always be in his company, he caused a bust of him to be executed by a first-rate artist, and to be placed in his own study, in order that Mr. Carlyle's image might be constantly present to his mind.* ,

---

by Oliver and Boyd ; and G. and W. B. Whittaker, London. 1824, pp. xvi., 367. Sir David Brewster's Preface, in which he speaks of "an Introduction on Proportion, by the Translator," is dated *Edinburgh, August* 1, 1822.

* See "Portraits of Public Characters," by the Author of "Random Recollections of the Lords and Commons." Lond. 1841, Vol. II., pp. 144, 158.

In 1823 Carlyle accepted the post of tutor to Charles Buller, of whose early death and honourable promise, two touching records remain to us, one in verse by Thackeray, and one in prose by Carlyle.

For the next four years Carlyle devoted his attention almost exclusively to German literature.

His Life of Schiller first appeared under the title of "Schiller's Life and Writings," in the London Magazine.

Part I.—October, 1823.

Part II.—January, 1824.

Part III.—July, 1824.

„        August, 1824.

„        September, 1824.

It was enlarged, and separately published by Messrs. Taylor and Hessey, the proprietors of the Magazine, in 1825.

The translation of "Wilhelm Meister," in 1824,* was the first real introduction of Goethe to the reading world of Great Britain. It appeared without the name of the translator, but its merits were too palpable to be overlooked, though some critics objected to

---

* Wilhelm Meister's Apprenticeship. 3 Vols., Edinburgh, 1824.

the strong infusion of German phraseology which had been imported into the English version. This acquired idiom never left our author, even in his original works, although the "Life of Schiller," written but a few months before, is almost entirely free from the peculiarity. "Wilhelm Meister," in its English dress, was better received by the English reading public than by English critics. De Quincey, in one of his dyspeptic fits, fell upon the book, its author, and the translator,* and Lord Jeffrey, in the Edinburgh Review, although admitting Carlyle to be a talented person, heaped condemnation upon the work.

Carlyle's next work was a series of translations, entitled "German Romance : Specimens of the chief Authors ; with Biographical and Critical Notices." 4 vols. Edinburgh, 1827. The Preface and Introductions are reprinted in the second volume of Carlyle's Collected Works : the Specimens translated from Hoffmann and La Motte Fouqué, have not been reprinted.

"This," says Carlyle, in 1857, "was a Book of

---

* Curiously enough in the very numbers of the "London Magazine" containing the later instalments of Carlyle's Life of Schiller.

Translations, not of my suggesting or desiring, but of my executing as honest journey-work in defect of better. The Pieces selected were the suitablest discoverable on such terms: not quite of *less* than no worth (I considered) any piece of them ; nor, alas, of a very high worth any, except one only. Four of these lots, or quotas to the adventure, Musäus's, Tieck's, Richter's, Goethe's, will be given in the final stage of this Series ; the rest we willingly leave, afloat or stranded, as waste driftwood, to those whom they may farther concern."

It was in 1826 that Mr. Carlyle married Miss Welsh, the only child of Dr. John Welsh, of Haddington,* a lineal descendant of John Knox, and a lady fitted in every way to be the wife of such a man. For a short time after marriage he continued to reside in Edinburgh, but during the following year he took up his residence in his native county, alternately at Comely Bank and Craigenputtoch—the latter a solitary farmhouse on a small estate he had acquired

---

* The noted Welsh of Ayr was a lineal ancestor of Carlyle's wife, and *he* now holds some property once actually belonging to that worthy. He had once made all preparations for writing Welsh's life, but gave up the project.

through his wife, about fifteen miles from Dumfries, and in one of the most secluded parts of the country. Most of his letters to Goethe were written from this place.

In one of the letters sent from Craigenputtoch to Weimar, bearing the date of 25th September, 1828, we have a charming picture of our author's seclusion and retired literary life at this period :—

"You inquire with such warm interest respecting our present abode and occupations, that I feel bound to say a few words about both, while there is still room left. Dumfries is a pleasant town, containing about fifteen thousand inhabitants, and may be con- sidered the centre of the trade and judicial system of a district which possesses some importance in the sphere of Scottish industry. Our residence is not in the town itself, but fifteen miles to the north-west, among the granite hills and the black morasses which stretch westward through Galloway, almost to the Irish Sea. In this wilderness of heath and rock, our estate stands forth a green oasis, a tract of ploughed, partly enclosed, and planted ground, where corn ripens, and trees afford a shade, although surrounded by sea-mews and rough-woolled sheep. Here, with no

small effort, have we built and furnished a neat, sub-
stantial dwelling ; here, in the absence of professorial
or other office, we live to cultivate literature according
to our strength, and in our own peculiar way.  We
wish a joyful growth to the rose and flowers of our
garden ; we hope for health and peaceful thoughts to
further our aims.  The roses, indeed, are still in part
to be planted, but they blossom already in anticipa-
tion.  Two ponies, which carry us everywhere, and
the mountain air, are the best medicines for weak
nerves.  This daily exercise—to which I am much
devoted—is my only recreation : for this nook of ours
is the loneliest in Britain—six miles removed from any
one likely to visit me.  Here Rousseau would have
been as happy as on his island of St. Pierre.  My
town friends, indeed, ascribe my sojourn here to a
similar disposition, and forbode me no good result.
But I came hither solely with the design to simplify
my way of life, and to secure the independence
through which I could be enabled to remain true to
myself.  This bit of earth is our own ; here we can
live, write, and think, as best pleases ourselves, even
though Zoilus himself were to be crowned the monarch
of literature.  Nor is the solitude of such great im-

portance; for a stage-coach takes us speedily to Edinburgh, which we look upon as our British Weimar.    And have I not, too, at this moment piled up upon the table of my little library a whole cart-load of French, German, American, and English journals and periodicals—whatever may be their worth ?   Of antiquarian studies, too, there is no lack. From some of our heights I can descry, about a day's journey to the west, the hill where Agricola and his Romans left a camp behind them.    At the foot of it I was born, and there both father and mother still live to love me.    And so one must let time work."

The above letter was printed by Goethe himself, in his Preface to a German translation of Carlyle's " Life of Schiller," published at Frankfort in 1830.    Other pleasant records of the intercourse between them exist in the shape of sundry graceful copies of verses addressed by Goethe to Mrs. Carlyle, which will be found in the collection of his poems.

Carlyle had now fairly started as an original writer. From the lonely farm of Craigenputtoch went forth the brilliant series of Essays published in the Edin-burgh, Westminster, and Foreign Quarterly Re-views, and in Fraser's Magazine, which were not

long in gaining for him a literary reputation in both
hemispheres. To this lonely farm came one day in
August, 1833, armed with a letter of introduction, a
visitor from the other side of the Atlantic : a young
American, then unknown to fame, by name Ralph
Waldo Emerson. The meeting of these two remarkable men was thus described by the younger of them,
many years afterwards :—

" I came from Glasgow to Dumfries, and being in-
tent on delivering a letter which I had brought from
Rome, inquired for Craigenputtoch. It was a farm in
Nithsdale, in the parish of Dunscore, sixteen miles
distant. No public coach passed near it, so I took a
private carriage from the inn. I found the house
amid desolate heathery hills, where the lonely scholar
nourished his mighty heart. Carlyle was a man from
his youth, an author who did not need to hide from
his readers, and as absolute a man of the world, unknown and exiled on that hill-farm, as if holding in
his own terms what is best in London. He was tall
and gaunt, with a cliff-like brow, self-possessed, and
holding his extraordinary powers of conversation in
easy command ; clinging to his northern accent with
evident relish ; full of lively anecdote, and with a

streaming humour, which floated everything he looked
upon.   His talk playfully exalting the familiar objects,
put the companion at once into an acquaintance with
his Lars and Lemurs, and it was very pleasant to learn
what was predestined to be a pretty mythology.   Few
were the objects and lonely the man, 'not a person to
speak to within sixteen miles except the minister of
Dunscore;' so that books inevitably made his topics.

  "He had names of his own for all the matters familiar to his discourse.   'Blackwood's' was the 'sand
magazine;' 'Fraser's' nearer approach to possibility
of life was the 'mud magazine;' a piece of road near
by that marked some failed enterprise was 'the grave
of the last sixpence.'   When too much praise of any
genius annoyed him, he professed hugely to admire
the talent shewn by his pig.   He had spent much time
and contrivance in confining the poor beast to one
enclosure in his pen, but pig, by great strokes of judgment, had found out how to let a board down, and
had foiled him.   For all that, he still thought man
the most plastic little fellow in the planet, and he liked
Nero's death, 'Qualis artifex pereo !' better than most
history.   He worships a man that will manifest any
truth to him.   At one time he had inquired and read

a good deal about America.   Landor's principle was
mere rebellion, and that he feared was the American
principle.   The best, thing he knew of that country
was, that in it a man can have meat for his labour.
He had read in Stewart's book, that when he had
inquired in a New York hotel for the Boots, he had
been shown across the street, and had found Mungo
in his own house dining on roast turkey.

"We talked of books.   Plato he does not read, and
he disparaged Socrates; and, when pressed, persisted
in making Mirabeau a hero.   Gibbon he called the
splendid bridge from the old world to the new.   His
own reading had been multifarious.   Tristram Shandy
was one of his first books after Robinson Crusoe, and
Robertson's America an early favourite.   Rousseau's
Confessions had discovered to him that he was not a
dunce; and it was now ten years since he had learned
German, by the advice of a man who told him he
would find in that language what he wanted.

"He took despairing or satirical views of literature
at this moment; recounted the incredible sums paid
in one year by the great booksellers for puffing.
Hence it comes that no newspaper is trusted now, no

books are bought, and the booksellers are on the eve of bankruptcy.

"He still returned to English pauperism, the crowded country, the selfish abdication by public men of all that public persons should perform. 'Government should direct poor men what to do. Poor Irish folk come wandering over these moors. My dame makes it a rule to give to every son of Adam bread to eat, and supplies his wants to the next house. But here are thousands of acres which might give them all meat, and nobody to bid these poor Irish go to the moor and till it. They burned the stacks, and so found a way to force the rich people to attend to them.'

"We went out to walk over long hills, and looked at Criffel, then without his cap, and down into Wordsworth's country. There we sat down, and talked of the immortality of the soul. It was not Carlyle's fault that we talked on that topic, for he had the natural disinclination of every nimble spirit to bruise itself against walls, and did not like to place himself where no step can be taken. But he was honest and true, and cognizant of the subtile links that bind ages together, and saw how every event affects all the future.

'Christ died on the tree : that built Dunscore kirk yonder : that brought you and me together. Time has only a relative existence.'

"He was already turning his eyes towards London with a scholar's appreciation. London is the heart of the world, he said, wonderful only from the mass of human beings. He liked the huge machine. Each keeps its own round. The baker's boy brings muffins to the window at a fixed hour every day, and that is all the Londoner knows, or wishes to know, on the subject. But it turned out good men. He named certain individuals, especially one man of letters, his friend, the best mind he knew, whom London had well served."* .

"Carlyle," says Emerson, "was already turning his eyes towards London," and a few months after the interview just described he did finally fix his residence there, in a quiet street in Chelsea, leading down to the river-side. Here, in an old-fashioned house, built in the reign of Queen Anne, he has lived ever since. Daniel Maclise, the distinguished artist, lives but a few doors off, around the corner at No. 4, Cheyne Walk.

* "English Traits," by R. W. Emerson. First Visit to England.

The artist made a portrait-sketch of his neighbour for "Fraser," in 1835.

With another man, of whom he now became the neighbour—Leigh Hunt—he had already formed a slight acquaintance, which soon ripened into a warm friendship and affection on both sides, in spite of their singular difference of temperament and character.

"It was on the 8th of February, 1832," says Mr. Thornton Hunt, "that the writer of the essays named 'Characteristics' received, apparently from Mr. Leigh Hunt, a volume entitled 'Christianism,' for which he begged to express his thanks. By the 20th of February, Carlyle, then lodging in London, was inviting Leigh Hunt to tea, as the means of their first meeting; and by the 20th of November, Carlyle wrote from Dumfries, urging Leigh Hunt to 'come hither and see us when you want to rusticate a month. Is that for ever impossible?' The philosopher afterwards came to live in the next street to his correspondent, in Chelsea, and proved to be one of Leigh Hunt's kindest, most faithful, and most considerate friends."*

* From "The Correspondence of Leigh Hunt," edited by his eldest son. London : Smith, Elder and Co. 1862. Vol. I., p. 321.

Mr. Horne tells a story very characteristic of both men. Soon after the publication of " Heroes and Hero Worship," they were at a small party, when a conversation was started between these two concerning the heroism of man. " Leigh Hunt had said something about the islands of the blest, or El Dorado, or the Millennium, and was flowing on his bright and hopeful way, when Carlyle dropped some heavy tree-trunk across Hunt's pleasant stream, and banked it up with philosophical doubts and objections at every interval of the speaker's joyous progress. But the unmitigated Hunt never ceased his overflowing anticipations, nor the saturnine Carlyle his infinite demurs to those finite flourishings. The listeners laughed and applauded by turns ; and had now fairly pitted them against each other, as the philosopher of hopefulness and of the unhopeful. The contest continued with all that ready wit and philosophy, that mixture of pleasantry and profundity, that extensive knowledge of books and character, with their ready application in argument or illustration, and that perfect ease and good nature which distinguish both of these men. The opponents were so well matched that it was quite clear the contest would never come to an end. But the night was far advanced, and the party broke up. They all sallied forth, and leaving the close room, the candles and the arguments behind them, suddenly found themselves in presence of a most brilliant starlight night.   They all looked up.   'Now,' thought Hunt, 'Carlyle's done for! he can have no answer to that!'   'There,' shouted Hunt, 'look up there, look at that glorious harmony, that sings with infinite voices an eternal song of Hope in the soul of man.'   Carlyle looked up.   They all remained silent to hear what he would say.   They began to think he was silenced at last—he was a mortal man.   But out of that silence came a few low-toned words, in a broad Scotch accent. And who on earth could have anticipated what the voice said?   'Eh! it's a sad sight!'   Hunt sat down on a stone step.   They all laughed—then looked very thoughtful.   Had the finite measured itself with infinity, instead of surrendering itself up to the influence?   Again they laughed—then bade each other good night, and betook themselves homeward with slow and serious pace."*

In 1840 Leigh Hunt left Chelsea, and went to live

* "A New Spirit of the Age," by R. H. Horne. London, 1844.  Vol. I. p. 278.

at Kensington, but Carlyle never altogether lost sight
of him, and on several occasions was able to do him
very serviceable acts of kindness ; as, for instance, in
writing certain memoranda concerning him with the
view of procuring from Government a small provision
for Leigh Hunt's declining years, which we may as
well give in this place :—

## MEMORANDA

### CONCERNING MR. LEIGH HUNT.

" 1. That Mr. Hunt is a man of the most indis-
putedly superior worth ; a *Man of Genius* in a very
strict sense of that word, and in all the senses which
it bears or implies ; of brilliant varied gifts, of graceful fertility, of clearness, lovingness, truthfulness ; of
childlike open character ; also of most pure and even
exemplary private deportment ; a man who can be
other than *loved* only by those who have not seen him,
or seen him from a distance through a false medium.

" 2. That, well seen into, he *has* done much for
the world ;—as every man possessed of such qualities,
and freely speaking them forth in the abundance of
his heart for thirty years long, must needs do : *how*

much, they that could judge best would perhaps estimate highest.

" 3. That, for one thing, his services in the cause
of reform, as Founder and long as Editor of the
' Examiner' newspaper; as Poet, Essayist, Public
Teacher in all ways open to him, are great and evident : few now living in this kingdom, perhaps, could
boast of greater.

" 4. That his sufferings in that same cause have
also been great ; legal prosecution and penalty (not
dishonourable to him ; nay, honourable, were the
whole truth known, as it will one day be) : unlegal
obloquy and calumny through the Tory Press ;—perhaps a greater quantity of baseness, persevering, im-
placable calumny, than any other living writer has
undergone. Which long course of hostility (nearly
the cruellest conceivable, had it not been carried on
in half, or almost total misconception) may be regarded
as the beginning of his other worst distresses, and a
main cause of them, down to this day.

" 5. That he is heavily laden with domestic bur-
dens, more heavily than most men, and his economical resources are gone from him. For the last twelve
years he has toiled continually, with passionate dili-

gence, with the cheerfullest spirit; refusing no task;
yet hardly able with all this to provide for the day
that was passing over him; and now, after some two
years of incessant effort in a new enterprise ('The
London Journal') that seemed of good promise, it
also has suddenly broken down, and he remains in
ill health, age creeping on him, without employment,
means, or outlook, in a situation of the painfullest
sort.    Neither do his distresses, nor did they at any
time, arise from wastefulness, or the like, on his own
part (he is a man of humble wishes, and can live with
dignity on little); but from crosses of what is called
Fortune, from injustice of other men, from inexpe-
rience of his own, and a guileless trustfulness of nature, the thing and things that have made him
unsuccessful make him in reality *more* loveable, and
plead for him in the minds of the candid.

" 6. That such a man is rare in a Nation, and of
high value there; not to be *procured* for a whole
Nation's revenue, or recovered when taken from us,
and some £200 a year is the price which this one,
whom we now have, is valued at; with that sum he
were lifted above his perplexities, perhaps saved from
nameless wretchedness !   It is believed that, in hardly

any other way could £200 abolish as much suffering, create as much benefit, to one man, and through him to many and all.

"Were these things set fitly before an English Minister, in whom great part of England recognises (with surprise at such a novelty) a man of insight, fidelity and decision, is it not probable or possible that he, though from a quite opposite point of view, might see them in somewhat of a similar light ; and, so seeing, determine to do in consequence? *Ut fiat!*

"T. C."

"Some years later," says a writer in " Macmillan's Magazine,"* "in the 'mellow evening' of a life that had been so stormy, Mr. Leigh Hunt himself told the story of his struggles, his victories, and his defeats, with so singularly graceful a frankness, that the most supercilious of critics could not but acknowledge that here was an autobiographer whom it was possible to like. Here is Mr. Carlyle's estimate of Hunt's Autobiography :—

* July, 1862.

"Chelsea, June 17, 1850.

"Dear Hunt,

"I have just finished your Autobiography, which has been most pleasantly occupying all my leisure these three days ; and you must permit me to write you a word upon it, out of the fulness of the heart, while the impulse is still fresh to thank you. This good book, in every sense one of the best I have read this long while, has awakened many old thoughts which never were extinct, or even properly asleep, but which (like so much else) have had to fall silent amid the tempests of an evil time—Heaven mend it ! A word from me once more, I know, will not be unwelcome, while the world is talking of you.

"Well, I call this an excellent good book, by far the best of the autobiographic kind I remember to have read in the English language ; and indeed, except it be Boswell's of Johnson, I do not know where we have such a picture drawn of a human life, as in these three volumes.

"A pious, ingenious, altogether human and worthy book; imaging, with graceful honesty and free feli-

city, many interesting objects and persons on your
life-path, and imaging throughout, what is best of all,
a gifted, gentle, patient, and valiant human soul, as
it buffets its way through the billows of time, and will
not drown though often in danger; cannot *be* drowned,
but conquers and leaves a track of radiance behind
it: that, I think, comes out more clearly to me than
in any other of your books;—and that, I can venture
to assure you, is the best of all results to readers in a
book of written record. In fact, this book has been
like a written exercise of devotion to me; I have not
assisted at any sermon, liturgy or litany, this long
while, that has had so religious an effect on me.
Thanks in the name of all men. And believe, along
with me, that this book will be welcome to other
generations as well as ours. And long may you live
to write more books for us; and may the evening sun
be softer on you (and on me) than the noon sometimes was!

"Adieu, dear Hunt (you must let me use this
familiarity, for I am now an old fellow too, as well as
you). I have often thought of coming up to see you
once more; and perhaps I shall, one of these days
(though there are such lions in the path, go whither-

ward one may) : but, whether I do or not, believe for ever in my regard. And so, God bless you,

> " Prays heartily,
>
> "T. CARLYLE."

On the other hand Leigh Hunt had an enthusiastic reverence for Carlyle. There are several incidental allusions to the latter, of more or less consequence, in Hunt's Autobiography, but the following is the most interesting :—

" *Carlyle's Paramount Humanity.*—I believe that what Mr. Carlyle loves better than his fault-finding, with all its eloquence, is the face of any human creature that looks suffering, and loving, and sincere ; and I believe further, that if the fellow-creature were suffering only, and neither loving nor sincere, but had come to a pass of agony in this life which put him at the mercies of some good man for some last help and consolation towards his grave, even at the risk of loss to repute, and a sure amount of pain and vexation, that man, if the groan reached him in its forlornness, would be Thomas Carlyle."*

* "Autobiography of Leigh Hunt, with Reminiscences of Friends and Contemporaries." (Lond. 1850.) Vol. III.

It was in " Leigh Hunt's Journal,"—a short-lived Weekly Miscellany (1850—1851) — that Carlyle's sketch, entitled " Two Hundred and Fifty Years Ago,"* first appeared.

It was during his residence in his Dumfries home that " Sartor Resartus " (" The Tailor Done Over," the name of an old Scotch ballad) was composed, which, after being rejected by several publishers, finally made its appearance in " Fraser's Magazine," 1833—34. The book—a five years' labour—might well have puzzled the critical gentlemen—the " book-tasters "— who decide for publishers what work to print among those submitted in manuscript. It is a sort of philo-sophical romance, in which the author undertakes to give, in the form of a review of a German work on dress, and in a notice of the life of the writer, his own opinions upon matters and things in general. The hero, Professor Teufelsdroeckh (" Devil's Dirt "), seems to be intended for a portrait of human nature as affected by the moral influence to which a cu...

* " Two Hundred and Fifty Years Ago. From a waste paper bag of T. Carlyle." Reprinted in Carlyle's Miscellanies, Ed. 1857.

vated mind would be exposed by the transcendental philosophy of Fichte. Mr. Carlyle works out his theory—the clothes philosophy—and finds the world false and hollow, our institutions mere worn-out rags or disguises, and that our only safety lies in flying from falsehood to truth, and becoming in harmony with the "divine idea." There is much fanciful, grotesque description in "Sartor," with deep thought and beautiful imagery.

With the publication of these papers in book form, "reprinted for friends," the next period in Mr. Carlyle's literary life may be said to begin.

"Sartor" found but few admirers; those readers, however, were firm and enthusiastic in their applause. In 1838 the "Sartor Resartus" papers, already republished in the United States, were issued in a collected form here; and in the same year his various scattered articles in periodicals, after having similarly received the honour of republication in America, were published here in five volumes, the articles being arranged in chronological order from 1827 to 1837, under the title of "Miscellanies."

It was in the spring of 1837 that our author's great historical work appeared, " The French Revolution :- -

Vol. I., The Bastile; Vol. II., The Constitution; Vol. III., The Guillotine." The publication of this work produced a profound impression on the public mind. A history abounding in vivid and graphic descriptions, it was at the same time a gorgeous prose epic. It is by far the ablest of all the author's works, and indeed is one of the most remarkable books of the age. There is no account of the French Revolution that can be compared with this for intensity of feeling and profoundness of thought.

A great deal of information respecting Carlyle's manner of living and personal history during these earlier years in London may be gleaned incidentally from his " Life of John Sterling," a book, which, from the nature of it, is necessarily partly autobiographical.

Thomas Moore and others met him sometimes in London society at this time. Moore thus briefly chronicles a breakfast at Lord Houghton's, at which Carlyle was present :—

" 22nd May, 1838.—Breakfasted at Milnes', and met rather a remarkable party, consisting of Savage, Landor, and Carlyle (neither of whom I had ever seen before), Robinson, Rogers, and Rice. A good deal of conversation between Robinson and Carlyle about German authors, of whom I knew nothing, nor (from what they paraded of them) felt that I had lost much by my ignorance."*

In 1835, after the publication of " Sartor Resartus," he received an invitation from several American admirers of his writings, to visit their country, and he contemplated doing so, but his labours in examining and collecting material for his great work on " The French Revolution," then hastening towards completion, prevented him.

We may say that, for many reasons, it is regrettable that this design was never carried into execution. Had Carlyle witnessed with his own eyes the admirable working of democratic institutions in the United States, he might have done more justice to our Transatlantic brethren, who were always his first and foremost admirers, and he might also have acquired more faith in the future destinies of his own countrymen.

In December, 1837, Carlyle wrote a very remarkable letter to a correspondent in India, which has

* Diary of Thomas Moore. (Lond. 1856.) vii., 224.

never been printed in his works, and which we are enabled to give here entire. It is addressed to Colonel David Lester Richardson, in acknowledgment of his "Literary Leaves, or Prose and Verse," published at Calcutta in 1836. These "Literary Leaves" contain among other things an article on the Italian opera (taking much the same view of it as Carlyle does), and a sketch of Edward Irving. These papers no doubt pleased Carlyle, and perhaps led him to entertain a rather exaggeratedly high opinion of the rest of the book.

### THOMAS CARLYLE TO DAVID LESTER RICHARDSON.

> "5, Cheyne Row, Chelsea, London,
> > "*19th December*, 1837.

"MY DEAR SIR,

"Your courteous gift, with the letter accompanying it, reached me only about a week ago, though dated 20th of June, almost at the opposite point of the year. Whether there has been undue delay or not is unknown to me, but at any rate on my side there ought to be no delay.

"I have read your volume—what little of it was

known to me before, and the much that was not known—I can say, with true pleasure. It is written, as few volumes in these days are, with fidelity, with successful care, with insight and conviction as to matter, with clearness and graceful precision as to manner: in a word, it is the impress of a mind stored with elegant accomplishments, gifted with an eye to see, and a heart to understand; a welcome, altogether recommendable book. More than once I have said to myself and others, How many parlour firesides are there this winter in England, at which this volume, could one give credible announcement of its quality, would be right pleasant company? There are very many, *could* one give the announcement: but no such announcement *can* be given; therefore the parlour firesides must even put up with . . . . . . or what other stuff chance shovels in their way, and read, though with malediction all the time. It is a great pity, but no man can help it. We are now arrived seemingly pretty near the point when all criticism and proclamation in matters literary has degenerated into an inane jargon, incredible, unintelligible, inarticulate as the cawing of choughs and rooks; and many things in that as in other provinces, are in a state of painful and rapid transition. A good book has no way of recommending itself except slowly and as it were accidentally from hand to hand. The man that wrote it must abide his time. He needs, as indeed all men do, the *faith* that this world is built not on falsehood and jargon but on truth and reason; that no good thing. done by any creature of God was, is, or ever can be *lost*, but will verily do the service appointed for it, and be found among the general sum-total and all of things after long times, nay after all time, and through eternity itself. Let him 'cast his bread upon the waters,' therefore, cheerful of heart; 'he will find it after many days.'

"I know not why I write all this to you; it comes very spontaneously from me. Let it be your satisfaction, the highest a man can have in this world, that the talent entrusted to you did not lie useless, but was turned to account, and proved itself to be a talent; and the 'publishing world' can receive it altogether according to their own pleasure, raise it high on the housetops, or trample it low into the street-kennels; that is not the question at all, the *thing* remains precisely what it was after never such raising and never such depressing and trampling, there is no change whatever in *it.* I bid you go on, and prosper.

"One thing grieves me: the tone of sadness, I might say of settled melancholy that runs through all your utterances of yourself. It is not right, it is wrong; and yet how shall I reprove you? If you knew me, you would triumphantly* for any spiritual endowment bestowed on a man, that it is accompanied, or one might say *preceded* as the first origin of it, always by a delicacy of organisation which in a world like ours is sure to have itself manifoldly afflicted, tormented, darkened down into sorrow and disease. You feel yourself an exile, in the East; but in the West too it is exile; I know not where under the sun it is not exile. Here in the Fog-Babylon, amid mud and smoke, in the infinite din of 'vociferous platitude,' and quack outbellowing quack, with truth and pity on all hands ground under the wheels, can one call it a home, or a world? It is a waste chaos, where we have to swim painfully for our life. The utmost a man can do is to swim there like a man, and hold his peace. For this seems to me a great truth, in any

* There seems to be a word omitted here by a slip of the pen.

exile or chaos whatsoever, that sorrow was not given us for sorrow's sake, but always and infallibly as a lesson to us from which we are to learn somewhat: and which, the somewhat once *learned*, ceases to be sorrow.   I do believe this ; and study in general to 'consume my own smoke,' not indeed without very ugly out-puffs at times !   Allan Cunningham is the best, he tells me that always as one grows older, one grows happier : a thing also which I really can believe. But as for you, my dear sir, you have other work to do in the East than grieve.   Are there not beautiful things there, glorious things ; wanting only an eye to note them, a hand to record them ?   If I had the command over you, I would say, read *Paul et Virginie*, then read the *Chaumière Indienne ;* gird yourself together for a right effort, and go and do likewise or better !   I mean what I say.   The East has its own phases, there are things there which the West yet knows not of; and one heaven covers both.   He that has an eye let him look !

"I hope you forgive me this style I have got into.   It seems to me on reading your book as if we had been long acquainted in some measure ; as if one might speak to you right from the heart.   I hope we shall

meet some day or other.   I send you my constant
respect and good wishes ; and am and remain,

"Yours very truly always,

"T. CARLYLE."

Carlyle first appeared as a lecturer in 1837.   His
first course was on 'German Literature,' at Willis's
Rooms ; a series of six lectures, of which the first was
thus noticed in the *Spectator* of Saturday, May 6, 1837·

"*Mr. Thomas Carlyle's Lectures.*

"Mr. Carlyle delivered the first of a course of
lectures ·on German Literature, at Willis's Rooms, on
Tuesday, to a very crowded and yet a select audience
of both sexes.   Mr. Carlyle may be deficient in the
mere mechanism of oratory ; but this minor defect is
far more than counterbalanced by his perfect mastery
of his subject, the originality of his manner, the perspicuity of his language, his simple but genuine
eloquence, and his vigorous grasp of a large and
difficult question.   No person of taste or judgment
could hear him without feeling that the lecturer is

---

* Facsimiled in "The Autographic Mirror," July, 1865.

3

a man of genius, deeply imbued with his great argument."

"This course of lectures," says a writer already
quoted, "was well attended by the fashionables of the
West End ; and though they saw in his manner some-.
thing exceedingly awkward, they could not fail to
discern in his matter the impress of a mind of great
originality and superior gifts."*

The following year he delivered a second course
on the 'History of Literature, or the Successive
Periods of European Culture,' at the Literary Insti-
tution in Edwards-street, Portman-square. 'The
Revolutions of Modern Europe' was the title given
to the third course, delivered twelve months
later. The fourth and last series, of six lectures, is
the best remembered, 'Heroes and Hero-worship.'
This course alone was published, and it became
more immediately popular than any of the works
which had preceded it. Concerning these lectures, Leigh Hunt remarked that it seemed "as
if some Puritan had come to life again, liberalized
by German philosophy and his own intense reflec-

* JAMES GRANT : "Portraits of Public Characters." (Lond.
1841.) Vol. ii., p. 152.

tions and experience." Another critic, a Scotch
writer, could see nothing but wild impracticability
in them, and exclaimed, " Can any living man point
to a single practical passage in any of these lectures ?  If not, what is the real value of Mr. Carlyle's
teachings ?  What is Mr. Carlyle himself but a
phantasm !"

The vein of Puritanism running through his writings,
composed upon the model of the German school,
impressed many critics with the belief that their
author, although full of fire and energy, was per-
plexed and embarrassed with his own speculations.
Concerning this Puritan element in his reflections,
Mr. James Hannay remarks, "That earnestness, that
grim humour—that queer, half-sarcastic, half-sympa-
thetic fun—is quite Scotch.  It appears in Knox
and Buchanan, and it appears in Burns.  I was not
surprised when a school-fellow of Carlyle's told me
that his favourite poem was, when a boy, ' Death and
Doctor  ornbook.'  And if I were asked to explain
this originality, I should say that he was a covenanter
coming in the wake of the eighteenth century and the
transcendental philosophy.  He has gone into the
hills against ' shams,' as they did against Prelacy,

Erastianism, and so forth.  But he lives in a quieter age, and in a literary position.  So he can give play to the humour which existed in them as well, and he overflows with a range of reading and speculation to which they were necessarily strangers."

'Chartism,' published in 1839, and which, to use the words of a critic of the time, was the publication in which "he first broke ground on the Condition of England question," appeared a short time before the lectures on 'Heroes and Hero-worship' were delivered.  If we remember rightly, Mr. Carlyle gave forth "those grand utterances" extemporaneously and without an abstract, notes, or a reminder of any kind—utterances not beautiful to the flunkey-mind, or valet-soul, occupied mainly with the fold of the hero's necktie, and the cut of his coat.  Flunkey-dom, by one of its mouthpieces, thus speaks of them :—

"Perhaps his course for the present year, which was on Hero-worship, was better attended than any previous one.  Some of those who were present estimated the average attendance at three hundred. They chiefly consisted of persons of rank and wealth, as the number of carriages which each day waited the conclusion of the lecture to receive Mr. Carlyle's auditors, and to carry them to their homes, conclusively testified.   The locality of Mr. Carlyle's lectures has, I believe, varied every year.   The Hanover Rooms, Willis's Rooms, and a place in the north of London, the name of which I forget, have severally been chosen as the place whence to give utterance to his profound and original trains of thought.

"A few words will be expected here as to Mr. Carlyle's manner as a lecturer.   In so far as his mere manner is concerned, I can scarcely bestow on him a word of commendation.   There is something in his manner which, if I may use a rather quaint term, must seem very uncouth to London audiences of the most respectable class, *accustomed as they are to the polished deportment\* which is usually exhibited in Willis's or the Hanover Rooms.*   When he enters the room, and proceeds to the sort of rostrum whence he delivers his lectures, he is, according to the usual practice in such cases, generally received with applause ; but he very rarely takes any more notice of the mark of approbation thus bestowed upon him, than if he were altogether unconscious of it.   And the same seeming want

* Shade of Mr. Turveydrop senior, hear this man !

of respect for his audience, or, at any rate, the same
disregard for what I believe he considers the trouble-
some forms of politeness, is visible at the commence-
ment of his lecture.    Having ascended his desk, he
gives a hearty rub to his hands, and plunges at once
into his subject.    He reads very closely, which, indeed, must be expected, considering the nature of the
topics which he undertakes to discuss.    He is not
prodigal of gesture with his arms or body ; but there
is something in his eye and countenance which indicates great earnestness of purpose, and the most intense interest in his subject.    *You can almost fancy,
in some of his more enthusiastic and energetic moments,
that you see his inmost soul in his face.*    At times, indeed very often, he so unnaturally distorts his features,
as to give to his countenance a very unpleasant expression.    On such occasions, you would imagine that
he was suddenly seized with some violent paroxysms
of pain.    *He is one of the most ungraceful speakers I
have ever heard address a public assemblage of persons.*
In addition to the awkwardness of his general manner,
he 'makes mouths,' which would of themselves be
sufficient to mar the agreeableness of his delivery.
And his manner of speaking, and the ungracefulness

of his gesticulation, are greatly aggravated by his strong Scotch accent. Even to the generality of Scotchmen his pronunciation is harsh in no ordinary degree. Need I say, then, what it must be to an English ear?

" I was present some months ago, during the delivery of a speech by Mr. Carlyle at a meeting held in the Freemasons' Tavern, for the purpose of forming a metropolitan library; and though that speech did not occupy in its delivery more than five minutes, he made use of some of the most extraordinary phraseology I ever heard employed by a human being. He made use of the expression 'this London,' which he pronounced 'this Loondun,' four or five times — a phrase which grated grievously on the ears even of those - of Mr. Carlyle's own countrymen who were present, and which must have sounded doubly harsh in the ears of an Englishman, considering the singularly broad Scotch accent with which he spoke.

" A good deal of uncertainty exists as to Mr. Carlyle's religious opinions. I have heard him represented as a firm and entire believer in revelation, and

I have heard it affirmed with equal confidence that he is a decided Deist.   My own impression is," &c.*

In 1841 Carlyle superintended the publication of the English edition of his friend Emerson's Essays,† to which he prefixed a characteristic Preface of some length. ˀ

"The name of Ralph Waldo Emerson," he writes, "is not entirely new in England : distinguished travellers bring us tidings of such a man ; fractions of his writings have found their way into the hands of the curious here ; fitful hints that there is, in New England, some spiritual notability called Emerson, glide through Reviews and Magazines.   Whether these hints were true or not true, readers are now to judge for themselves a little better.

"Emerson's writings and speakings amount to something : and yet hitherto, as seems to me, this Emerson is perhaps far less notable for what he has spoken or

* "Portraits of Public Characters," by the author of "Random Recollections of the Lords and Commons." Vol. ii. pp. 152—158.

† Essays : by R. W. Emerson, of Concord, Massachusetts. With Preface by Thomas Carlyle.   London : James Fraser. 1841.

done, than for the many things he has not spoken and has forborne to do.   With uncommon interest I have learned that this, and in such a never-resting, locomotive country too, is one of those rare men who have withal the invaluable talent of sitting still !   That an educated man, of good gifts and opportunities, after looking at the public arena, and even trying, not with ill success, what its tasks and its prizes might amount to, should retire for long years into rustic obscurity ; and, amid the all-pervading jingle of dollars and loud chaffering of ambitions and promotions, should quietly, with cheerful deliberateness, sit down to spend *his* life not in Mammon-worship, or the hunt for reputation, influence, place, or any outward advantage whatsoever : this, when we get a notice of it, is a thing really worth noting."

In 1843, "Past and Present" appeared—a work without the wild power which "Sartor Resartus" possessed over the feelings of the reader, but containing passages which look the same way, and breathe the same spirit.   The book contrasts, in a historico-philosophical spirit, English society in the Middle Ages, with English society in our own day.   In both this and the preceding work the great measures advised for the amelioration of the people are education and emigration.

Another very admirable letter, addressed by Mr. Carlyle in 1843 to a young man who had written to him desiring his advice as to a proper choice of reading, and, it would appear also, as to his conduct in general, we shall here bring forth from its hiding-place in an old Scottish newspaper of a quarter of a century ago :—

" DEAR SIR,

"SOME time ago your letter was delivered me ; I take literally the first free half-hour I have had since to write you a word of answer.

"It would give me true satisfaction could any advice of mine contribute to forward you in your honourable course of self-improvement, but a long experience has taught me that advice can profit but little ; that there is a good reason why advice is so seldom followed ; this reason namely, that it so seldom, and can almost never be, rightly given. No man knows the state of another; it is always to some more or less imaginary man that the wisest and most honest adviser is speaking.

" As to the books which you—whom I know so little of—should read, there is hardly anything definite that can be said.   For one thing, you may be strenuously advised to keep reading.   Any good book, any book that is wiser than yourself, will teach you something—a great many things, indirectly and directly, if your mind be open to learn.   This old counsel of Johnson's is also good, and universally applicable :— ' Read the book you do honestly feel a wish and curiosity to read.'   The very wish and curiosity indicates that you, then and there, are the person likely to get good of it.   ' Our wishes are presentiments of our capabilities ;' that is a noble saying, of deep encouragement to all true men ; applicable to our wishes and efforts in regard to reading as to other things. Among all the objects that look wonderful or beautiful to you, follow with fresh hope the one which looks wonderfullest, beautifullest.   You will gradually find, by various trials (which trials see that you make honest, manful ones, not silly, short, fitful ones), what *is* for you the wonderfullest, beautifullest—what is *your* true element and province, and be able to profit by that.   True desire, the monition of nature, is much to be attended to.   But here, also, you are to discriminate carefully between *true* desire and false. The medical men tell us we should eat what we *truly* have an appetite for; but what we only *falsely* have an appetite for we should resolutely avoid. It is very true; and flimsy, desultory readers, who fly from foolish book to foolish book, and get good of none, and mischief of all—are not these as foolish, unhealthy eaters, who mistake their superficial false desire after spiceries and confectioneries for their real appetite, of which even they are not destitute, though it lies far deeper, far quieter, after solid nutritive food? With these illustrations, I will recommend Johnson's advice to you.

"Another thing, and only one other, I will say. All books are properly the record of the history of past men—what thoughts past men had in them—what actions past men did: the summary of all books whatsoever lies there. It is on this ground that the class of books specifically named History can be safely recommended as the basis of all study of books —the preliminary to all right and full understanding of anything we can expect to find in books. Past history, and especially the past history of one's own native country, everybody may be advised to begin with that. Let him study that faithfully; innumerable inquiries will branch out from it; he has a broad-beaten highway, from which all the country is more or less visible ; there travelling, let him choose where he will dwell.

"Neither let mistakes and wrong directions—of which every man, in his studies and elsewhere, falls into many—discourage you. There is precious instruction to be got by finding that we are wrong. Let a man try faithfully, manfully, to be right, he will grow daily more and more right. It is, at bottom, the condition which all men have to cultivate themselves. Our very walking is an incessant falling—a falling and a catching of ourselves before we come actually to the pavement!—it is emblematic of all things a man does.

"In conclusion, I will remind you that it is not books alone, or by books chiefly, that a man becomes in all points a man. Study to do faithfully whatsoever thing in your actual situation, there and now, you find either expressly or tacitly. laid to your charge ; that is your post ; stand in it like a true soldier. Silently devour the many chagrins of it, as all human situations have many ; and see you aim not to quit it without doing all that *it*, at least, required of you.  A man perfects himself by work much more than by reading. They are a growing kind of men that can wisely combine the two things—wisely, valiantly, can do what is laid to their hand in their present sphere, and prepare themselves withal for doing other wider things, if such lie before them.

"With many good wishes and encouragements, I remain, yours sincerely,

"THOMAS CARLYLE.

"Chelsea, 13th March, 1843."

The publication of "Past and Present" elicited a paper "On the Genius and Tendency of the Writings of Thomas Carlyle," from Mazzini, which appeared in the "British and Foreign Review," of October, 1843.* It is a candid and thoughtful piece of criticism, in which the writer, while striving to do justice to Carlyle's genius, protests strongly and uncompromisingly against the tendency of his teaching.

Some months afterwards, when the House of Commons was occupied with the illegal opening of

---

* Reprinted in the "Life and Writings of Joseph Mazzini." (London, 1867).  Vol. iv. pp. 56—144.

Mazzini's letters, Carlyle spontaneously stepped forward and paid the following tribute to his character :—

"TO THE EDITOR OF THE 'TIMES.'

"SIR,—

"IN your observations in yesterday's *Times* on the late disgraceful affair of Mr. Mazzini's letters and the Secretary of State, you mention that Mr. Mazzini is entirely unknown to you, entirely indifferent to you ; and add, very justly, that if he were the most contemptible of mankind, it would not affect your argument on the subject.*

"It may tend to throw farther light on this matter if I now certify you, which I in some sort feel called upon to do, that Mr. Mazzini is not unknown to various competent persons in this country ; and that he

---

* "Mr. Mazzini's character and habits and society are nothing to the point, unless connected with some certain or probable evidence of evil intentions or treasonable plots. We know nothing, and care nothing about him. He may be the most worthless and the most vicious creature in the world ; but this is no reason of itself why his letters should be detained and opened."— *Times'* leading article, June 17, 1844.

is very far indeed from being contemptible—none
farther, or very few of living men. I have had the
honour to know Mr. Mazzini for a series of years;
and, whatever I may think of his practical insight and
skill in worldly affairs, I can with great freedom testify
to all men that he, if I have ever seen one such, is a
man of genius and virtue, a man of sterling veracity,
humanity, and nobleness of mind; one of those rare
men, numerable unfortunately but as units in this
world, who are worthy to be called martyr-souls; who,
in silence, piously in their daily life, understand and
practise what is meant by that.

"Of Italian democracies and young Italy's sorrows,
of extraneous Austrian Emperors in Milan, or poor
old chimerical Popes in Bologna, I know nothing, and
desire to know nothing; but this other thing I do
know, and can here declare publicly to be a fact,
which fact all of us that have occasion to comment on
Mr. Mazzini and his affairs may do well to take along
with us, as a thing leading towards new clearness, and
not towards new additional darkness, regarding him
and them.

"Whether the extraneous Austrian Emperor and
miserable old chimera of a Pope shall maintain them-

selves in Italy, or be obliged to decamp from Italy, is
not a question in the least vital to Englishmen. But
it is a question vital to us that sealed letters in an English post-office be, as we all fancied they were,
respected as things sacred ; that opening of men's
letters, a practice near of kin to picking men's pockets,
and to other still viler and far fataler forms of scoundrelism, be not resorted to in England, except in cases
of the very last extremity. When some new gun-
powder plot may be in the wind, some double-
dyed high treason, or imminent national wreck not
avoidable otherwise, then let us open letters—not
till then.

"To all Austrian Kaisers and such like, in their
time of trouble, let us answer, as our fathers from of
old have answered :—Not by such means is help here
for you. Such means, allied to picking of pockets
and viler forms of scoundrelism, are not permitted in
this country for your behoof. The right hon. Secretary does himself detest such, and even is afraid to
employ them. He dare not : it would be dangerous
for him ! All British men that might chance to come
in view of such a transaction, would incline to spurn

4

it, and trample on it, and indignantly ask him what he meant by it ?

        " I am, Sir, your obedient servant,

                " THOMAS CARLYLE.*

" Chelsea, June 18."

The autumn of this year was saddened for Carlyle by the loss of the dear friend whose biography he afterwards wrote.   On the 18th of September, 1844— after a short career of melancholy promise, only half fulfilled — John Sterling died, in his thirty-ninth year.

The next work that appeared from his pen—a special service to history, and to the memory of one of England's greatest men—was " Oliver Cromwell's Letters and Speeches, with Elucidations and a Connecting Narrative," two volumes, published in 1845. If there were any doubt remaining after the publication of the " French Revolution" what position our author might occupy amongst the historians of the age, it was fully removed on the appearance of " Cromwell's Letters."   The work obtained a great and an immediate popularity ; and though bulky and expen-

    * From *The Times*, Wednesday, June 19, 1844.

sive, a very large impression was quickly sold. These speeches and letters of Cromwell, the spelling and punctuation corrected, and a few words added here and there for clearness' sake, and to accommodate them to the language and style in use now, were first made intelligible and effective by Mr. Carlyle. "The authentic utterances of the man Oliver himself," he says, "I have gathered them from far and near; fished them up from the foul Lethean quagmires where they lay buried. I have washed, or endeavoured to wash them clean from foreign stupidities—such a job of buckwashing as I do not long to repeat—and the world shall now see them in their own shape." The work was at once republished in America, and two editions were called for here within the year.

While engaged on this work, Carlyle went down to Rugby by express invitation, on Friday, 13th May, 1842, and on the following day explored the field of Naseby, in company with Dr. Arnold. The meeting of two such remarkable men—only six weeks before the death of the latter—has in it something solemn and touching, and unusually interesting. Carlyle left the school-house, expressing the hope that it might "long continue to be what was to him one of the rarest sights in the world—a temple of industrious peace."

Arnold, who, with the deep sympathy arising from kindred nobility of soul, had long cherished a high reverence for Carlyle, was very proud of having received such a guest under his roof, and during those few last weeks of life was wont to be in high spirits, talking with his several guests, and describing with much interest, his recent visit to Naseby with Carlyle, " its position on some of the highest table-land in England—the streams falling on the one side into the Atlantic, on the other into the German Ocean—far away, too, from any town—Market Harborough, the nearest, into which the cavaliers were chased late in the long summer evening on the fourteenth of June."

Perhaps the most graphic description of Carlyle's manner and conversation ever published, is contained in the following passage from a letter addressed to Emerson by an accomplished American, Margaret Fuller, who visited England in the Autumn of 1846, and whose strange, beautiful history and tragical death on her homeward voyage, are known to most readers.

The letter is dated Paris, November 16, 1846.

"Of the people I saw in London, you will wish me to speak first of the Carlyles. Mr. C. came to see me at once, and appointed an evening to be passed at their house. That first time, I was delighted with him. He was in a very sweet humour, —full of wit and pathos, without being overbearing or oppressive. I was quite carried away with the rich flow of his discourse, and the hearty, noble earnestness of his personal being brought back the charm which once was upon his writing, before I wearied of it. I admired his Scotch, his way of singing his great full sentences, so that each one was like the stanza of a narrative ballad. He let me talk, now and then, enough to free my lungs and change my position, so that I did not get tired. That evening, he talked of the present state of things in England, giving light, witty sketches of the men of the day, fanatics and others, and some sweet, homely stories he told of things he had known of the Scotch peasantry.

"Of you he spoke with hearty kindness; and he told, with beautiful feeling, a story of some poor

farmer, or artisan in the country, who on Sunday
lays aside the cark and care of that dirty English
world, and sits reading the Essays, and looking upon
the sea.

"I left him that night, intending to go out very
often to their house. I assure you there never was
anything so witty as Carlyle's description of ——
——. It was enough to kill one with laughing. I,
on my side, contributed a story to his fund of anecdote on this subject, and it was fully appreciated.
Carlyle is worth a thousand of you for that ;—he is
not ashamed to laugh when he is amused, but goes on
in a cordial, human fashion.

"The second time Mr. C. had a dinner-party, at
which was a witty, French, flippant sort of man,
author of a History of Philosophy,* and now writing
a Life of Goethe, a task for which he must be as
unfit as irreligion and sparkling shallowness can make
him. But he told stories admirably, and was allowed
sometimes to interrupt Carlyle a little, of which
one was glad, for that night he was in his more
acrid mood, and though much more brilliant than

* George Henry Lewes.

on the former evening, grew wearisome to me, who disclaimed and rejected almost everything he said.

"For a couple of hours he was talking about poetry, and the whole harangue was one eloquent proclamation of the defects in his own mind. Tennyson wrote in verse because the schoolmasters had taught him that it was great to do so, and had thus, unfortunately, been turned from the true path for a man. Burns had, in like manner, been turned from his vocation. Shakspeare had not had the good sense to see that it would have been better to write straight on in prose;—and such nonsense, which, though amusing enough at first, he ran to death after a while.

"The most amusing part is always when he comes back to some refrain, as in the French Revolution of the *sea-green*. In this instance, it was Petrarch and *Laura*, the last word pronounced with his ineffable sarcasm of drawl. Although he said this over fifty times, I could not help laughing when *Laura* would come. Carlyle running his chin out when he spoke it, and his eyes glancing till they looked like the eyes and beak of a bird of prey.

Poor Laura ! Luckily for her that her poet had already got her safely canonized beyond the reach of this Teufelsdröckh vulture.

" The worst of hearing Carlyle is, that you cannot interrupt him. I understand the habit and power of haranguing have increased very much upon him, so that you are a perfect prisoner when he has once got hold of you. To interrupt him is a physical impossibility. If you get a chance to remonstrate for a moment, he raises his voice and bears you down. True, he does you no injustice, and, with his admirable penetration, sees the disclaimer in your mind, so that you are not morally delinquent ; but it is not pleasant to be unable to utter it. The latter part of the evening, however, he paid us for this, by a series of sketches, in his finest style of railing and raillery, of modern French literature, not one of them, perhaps, perfectly just, but all drawn with the finest, boldest strokes, and, from his point of view, masterly. All were depreciating, except that of Béranger. Of him he spoke with perfect justice, because with hearty sympathy.

" I had, afterward, some talk with Mrs. C., whom hitherto I had only *seen*, for who can speak while her

husband is there ?   I like her very much ;—she is full
of grace, sweetness, and talent.   Her eyes are sad
and charming.

.

" After this, they went to stay at Lord Ashburton's,
and I only saw them once more, when they came to
pass an evening with us.   Unluckily, Mazzini was
with us, whose society, when he was there alone, I
enjoyed more than any.   He is a beauteous and pure
music : also, he is a dear friend of Mrs. C., but his
being there gave the conversation a turn to 'progress' and ideal subjects, and C. was fluent in invec-
tives on all our 'rose-water imbecilities.'   We all felt
distant from him, and Mazzini, after some vain efforts
to remonstrate, became very sad.   Mrs. C. said to
me,—

" ' These are but opinions to Carlyle, but to Mazzini, who has given his all, and helped bring his
friends to the scaffold, in pursuit of such subjects, it
is a matter of life and death.'

" All Carlyle's talk, that evening, was a defence of
mere force,—success the test of right ;—if people
would not behave well, put collars round their necks ;
—find a hero, and let them be his slaves, &c.   It

was very Titanic, and anti-celestial. I wish the last evening had been more melodious. However, I bid Carlyle farewell with feelings of the warmest friendship and admiration. We cannot feel otherwise to a great ·and noble nature, whether it harmonise with our own or not. I never appreciated the work he has done for his age till I saw England. I could not. You must stand in the shadow of that mountain of shams, to know how hard it is to cast light across it.

"Honour to Carlyle! *Hoch!* Although, in the wine with which we drink this health, I, for one, must mingle the despised ' rose-water.'

"And now, having to your eye shown the defects of my own mind, in the sketch of another, I will pass on more lowly,—more willing to be imperfect, since Fate permits such noble creatures, after all, to be only this or that. It is much if one is not only a crow or magpie ;—Carlyle is only a lion. Some time we may, all in full, be intelligent and humanely fair."

"*December*, 1846.—Accustomed to the infinite wit and exuberant richness of his writings, his talk is still an amazement and a splendour scarcely to be faced with steady eyes. He does not converse ;— only harangues. It is the usual misfortune of such marked men,—happily not one invariable or inevitable,—that they cannot allow other minds room to breathe, and show themselves in their atmosphere, and thus miss the refreshment and instruction which the greatest never cease to need from the experience of the humblest.

" Carlyle allows no one a chance, but bears down all opposition, not only by his wit and onset of words, resistless in their sharpness as so many bayonets, but by actual physical superiority,—raising his voice, and rushing on his opponent with a torrent of sound. This is not in the least from unwillingness to allow freedom to others. On the contrary, no man would more enjoy a manly resistance to his thought. But it is the impulse of a mind accustomed to follow out its own impulse, as the hawk its prey, and which knows not how to stop in the chase. Carlyle, indeed, is arrogant and overbearing ; but in his arrogance there is no littleness,—no self-love. It is the heroic arrogance of some old Scandinavian conqueror ;—it is his nature, and the untameable impulse that has given him power to crush the dragons. You do not love him, perhaps, nor revere; and perhaps, also, he would only laugh at you if you did; but you like him heartily, and like to see him the powerful smith, the Siegfried, melting all the old iron in his furnace till it glows to a sunset red, and burns you, if you senselessly go too near.

"He seems, to me, quite isolated,—lonely as the desert,—yet never was a man more fitted to prize a man, could he find one to match his mood. He finds them, but only in the past. He sings, rather. than talks. He pours upon you a kind of satirical, heroical, critical poem, with regular cadences, and generally catching up, near the beginning, some singular epithet, which serves as a *refrain* when his song is full, or with which, as with a knitting needle, he catches up the stitches, if he has chanced, now and then, to let fall a row.

"For the higher kinds of poetry he has no sense, and his talk on that subject is delightfully and gorgeously absurd. He sometimes stops a minute to laugh at it himself, then begins anew with fresh vigour; for all the spirits he is driving before him

seem to him as Fata Morganas, ugly masks, in fact,
if he can but make them turn about; but he laughs
that they seem to others such dainty Ariels.   His
talk, like his books, is full of pictures; his critical
strokes masterly.  Allow for his point of view, and
his survey is admirable.  He is a large subject.   I
cannot speak more or wisclier of him now, nor needs
it ;—his works are true, to blame and praise him,—
the Siegfried of England,—great and powerful, if not
quite invulnerable, and of a might rather to destroy
evil, than legislate for good."*

In 1848 Mr. Carlyle contributed a series of articles to the *Examiner* and *Spectator*, principally on
Irish affairs, which, as he has never yet seen fit to
reprint them in his Miscellanies, are apparently quite
unknown to the general public.   With the exception of the last, they may be considered as a sort
of alarum note, sounded to herald the approach
of the Latter-Day Pamphlets, which appeared shortly
afterwards.

* "Memoirs of Margaret Fuller Ossoli." (Boston, 1852.)
Vol. iii., pp. 96—104.

The following is a list of these newspaper articles :—

In *The Examiner*, 1848.

      March 4.    "Louis Philippe."
      April 29.    "Repeal of the Union."
      May 13.    "Legislation for Ireland."

In *The Spectator*, 1848.

      May 13.    "Ireland and the British Chief
                 Governor."
          ,,    "Irish Regiments (of the New
                 Era)."

In *The Examiner*, 1848.

    Dec. 2.   "Death of Charles Buller."

The last-named paper, a tribute to the memory of
his old pupil, we shall give entire. Another man of
genius,* now also gone to his rest, sang sorrowfully
on the same occasion :

    "Who knows the inscrutable design?
      Blest be He who took and gave !
    Why should your mother, Charles, not mine,
      Be weeping at her darling's grave?

        * W. M. Thackeray.

We bow to Heaven that will'd it so,
That darkly rules the fate of all,
That sends the respite or the blow,
That's free to give, or to recall."

Carlyle's paper reads like a solemn and touching funeral oration to the uncovered mourners as they stand round the grave before it is closed :—

" A very beautiful soul has suddenly been summoned from among us ; one of the clearest intellects, and most aërial activities in England, has unexpectedly been called away.  Charles Buller died on Wednesday morning last, without previous sickness, reckoned of importance, till a day or two before. An event of unmixed sadness, which has created a just sorrow, private and public.  The light of many a social circle is dimmer henceforth, and will miss long a presence which was always gladdening and beneficent; in the coming storms of political trouble, which heap themselves more and more in ominous clouds on our horizon, one radiant element is to be wanting now.

"Mr. Buller was in his forty-third year, and had sat in Parliament some twenty of those.  A man

long kept under by the peculiarities of his endowment
and position, but rising rapidly into importance of
late years; beginning to reap the fruits of long patience, and to see an ever wider field open round
him.      He was what in party language is called a
'Reformer,' from his earliest youth; and never
swerved from that faith, nor could swerve.      His luminous sincere intellect laid bare to him in all its ab-
ject incoherency the thing that was untrue, which
thenceforth became for him a thing that was not
tenable, that it was perilous and scandalous to attempt maintaining.      Twenty years in the dreary,
weltering lake of parliamentary confusion, with its
disappointments and bewilderments, had not quenched
this tendency, in which, as we say, he persevered as
by a law of nature itself, for the essence of his mind
was clearness, healthy purity, incompatibility with
fraud in any of its forms.      What he accomplished,
therefore, whether great or little, was all to be *added*
to the sum of good; none of it to be deducted.
There shone mildly in his whole conduct a beautiful
veracity, as if it were unconscious of itself; a perfect
spontaneous absence of all cant, hypocrisy, and hollow pretence, not in word and act only, but in

thought and ₁nstinct.   To a singular extent it can be
said of him ᵢthat he was a spontaneous clear man.
Very gentle, too, though full of fire; simple, brave,
graceful.   What he did, and what he said, came from
him as light from a luminous body, and had thus
always in it a high and rare merit, which any of the
more discerning could appreciate fully.

"To many, for a long while, Mr. Buller passed
merely for a man of wit, and certainly his beautiful
natural gaiety of character, which by no means meant
*levity*, was commonly thought to mean it, and did for
many years, hinder the recognition of his intrinsic
higher qualities.   Slowly it began to be discovered
that, under all this many-coloured radiancy and corus-
cation, there burnt a most steady light; a sound,
penetrating intellect, full of adroit resources, and
loyal by nature itself to all that was methodic, manful, true;—in brief, a mildly resolute, chivalrous,
and gallant character, capable of doing much serious
service.

"A man of wit he indisputably was, whatever more;
amongst the wittiest of men.   His speech, and manner of being, played everywhere like soft brilliancy
of lambent fire round the common objects of the

hour, and was, beyond all others that English society could show, entitled to the name of excellent, for it was spontaneous, like all else in him, genuine, humane,—the glittering play of the soul of a real man. To hear him, the most serious of men might think within himself, ' How beautiful is human gaiety too !' Alone of wits, Buller never made wit ; he could be silent, or grave enough, where better was going ; often rather liked to be silent if permissible, and always was so where needful. His wit, moreover, was ever the ally of wisdom, not of folly, or unkindness, or injustice ; no soul was ever hurt by it ; never, we believe, never, did his wit offend justly any man, and often have we seen his ready resource relieve one ready to be offended, and light up a pausing circle all into harmony again. In truth, it was beautiful to see such clear, almost childlike simplicity of heart co-existing with the finished dexterities, and long experiences, of a man of the world. Honour to human worth, in whatever form we find it ! This man was true to his friends, true to his convictions,—and true without effort, as the magnet is to the north. He was ever found on the right side ; helpful to it, not obstructive of it, in all he attempted or performed.

" Weak health; a faculty indeed brilliant, clear, prompt, not deficient in depth either, or in any kind of active valour, but wanting the stern energy that could long endure to *continue* in the deep, in the chaotic, new, and painfully incondite—this marked out for him his limits; which, perhaps with regrets enough, his natural veracity and practicality would lead him quietly to admit and stand by.  He was not the man to grapple, in its dark and deadly dens, with the Lernæan coil of social Hydras; perhaps not under any circumstances: but he did, unassisted, what he could; faithfully himself did something—nay, something truly considerable;—and in his *patience* with the much that by him and his strength could not be done let us grant there was something of beautiful too !

" Properly, indeed, his career as a public man was but beginning.  In the office he last held, much was silently expected of him; he himself, too, recognised well what a fearful and immense question this of Pauperism is; with what ominous rapidity the demand for solution of it is pressing on; and how little the world generally is yet aware what methods and principles, new, strange, and altogether contradictory to·

the shallow maxims and idle philosophies current at present, would be needed for dealing with it! This task he perhaps contemplated with apprehension ; but he is not now to be tried with this, or with any task more. He has fallen, at this point of the march, an honourable soldier ; and has left us here to fight along without him. Be his memory dear and honourable to us, as that of one so worthy ought. What in him was true and valiant endures for evermore—beyond all memory or record. His light, airy brilliancy has suddenly become solemn, fixed in the earnest stillness of Eternity. *There* shall we also, and our little works, all shortly be."

In 1850 appeared the "Latter-Day Pamphlets," essays suggested by the convulsions of 1848, in which, more than in any previous publication, the author spoke out in the character of a social and political censor of his own age. "He seemed to be the worshipper of mere brute force, the advocate of all harsh, coercive measures. Model prisons and schools for the reform of criminals, poor-laws, churches as at present constituted, the aristocracy, parliament, and other institutions, were assailed and ridiculed in unmeasured terms, and generally, the English public was

set down as composed of sham heroes, and a valet
or ' flunkey' world."   From their very nature as stern
denunciations of what the author considered contemporary fallacies, wrongs, and hypocrisies, these pamphlets produced a storm of critical indignation against
the author.

The Life of John Sterling was published in the
following year ; and our author then began that long
spell of work—the " History of Frederick the Great"
—which extended over fourteen years, the last, and
perhaps the greatest, monument of his genius.

In 1856, when we may suppose his mind to be full
of the details of battles, and overflowing with military
tactics, he received from Sir W. Napier his " History
of the Administration of Scinde," and wrote the following letter to the author :—

"THOMAS CARLYLE TO SIR WILLIAM NAPIER.

"Chelsea, May 12, 1856.

" DEAR SIR,

"I HAVE read with attention, and with many
feelings and reflections, your record of Sir C. Napier's
Administration of Scinde.   You must permit me to

thank you, in the name of Britain at large, for writing such a book ; and in my own poor name to acknowledge the great compliment and kindness implied in sending me a copy for myself.

" It is a book which every living Englishman would be the better for reading—for studying diligently till he saw into it, till he recognised and believed the high and tragic phenomenon set forth there ! A book which may be called 'profitable' in the old Scripture sense; profitable for reproof, for correction and admonition, for great sorrow, yet for 'building up in righteousness' too—in heroic, manful endeavour to do well, and not ill, in one's time and place. One feels it a kind of possession to know that one has had such a fellow-citizen and contemporary in these evil days.

" The fine and noble qualities of the man are very recognisable to me ; his subtle, piercing intellect turned all to the practical, giving him just insight into men and into things ; his inexhaustible adroit contrivances; his fiery valour; sharp promptitude to seize the good moment that will not return. A lynx-eyed, fiery man, with the spirit of an old knight in him ;

more of a hero than any modern I have seen for a long time.

"A singular veracity one finds in him ; not in his words alone—which, however, I like much for their fine rough *naïveté*—but in his actions, judgments, aims ; in all that he thinks, and does, and says— which, indeed, I have observed is the root of all greatness or real worth in human creatures, and properly the first (and also the rarest) attribute of what we call *genius* among men.

"The path of such a man through the foul jungle of this world—the struggle of Heaven's inspiration against the terrestrial fooleries, cupidities, and cowardices—cannot be other than tragical : but the man does tear out a bit of way for himself too ; strives towards the good goal, inflexibly persistent till his long rest come : the man does leave his mark behind him, ineffaceable, beneficent to all good men, maleficent to none : and we must not complain.    The British nation of this time, in India or elsewhere—God knows no nation ever had more need of such men, in every region of its affairs !  But also perhaps no nation ever had a much worse chance to get hold of them, to

recognise and loyally second them, even when they
are there.

"Anarchic stupidity is wide as the night; victorious
wisdom is but as a lamp in it shining here and there.
Contrast a Napier even in Scinde with, for example, a
Lally at Pondicherry or on the Place de Grève; one
has to admit that it is the common lot, that it might
have been far worse !

"There is great talent in this book apart from its
subject. The narrative moves on with strong, weighty
step, like a marching phalanx, with the gleam of clear
steel in it—sheers down the opponent objects and
tramples them out of sight in a very potent manner.
The writer, it is evident, had in him a lively, glowing
image, complete in all its parts, of the transaction to
be told; and that is his grand secret of giving the
reader so lively a conception of it. · I was surprised
to find how much I had carried away with me, even
of the Hill campaign and of Trukkee itself; though
without a map the attempt to understand such a thing
seemed to me desperate at first.

"With many thanks, and gratified to have made
this reflex acquaintance, which, if it should ever

chance to become a direct one, might gratify me still more,

"I remain always yours sincerely,

"T. CARLYLE."*

In June, 1861, a few days after the great fire in which Inspector Braidwood perished in the discharge of his duty, Carlyle broke a long silence with the following letter :—

"TO THE EDITOR OF THE 'TIMES.'

"SIR,—

"There is a great deal of public sympathy, and of deeper sort than usual, awake at present on the subject of Inspector Braidwood. It is a beautiful emotion, and apparently a perfectly just one, and well bestowed. Judging by whatever light one gets, Braidwood seems to have been a man of singular worth in his department, and otherwise; such a servant as the public seldom has. Thoroughly skilled in his function, nobly valiant in it, and faithful to it—

* "Life of General Sir William Napier, K.C.B." Edited by H. A. Bruce, M.P.   London : Murray, 1864.   Vol. II. pp. 312—314.

faithful to the death.    In rude, modest form, actually
a kind of hero, who has perished in serving us !

"Probably  his  sorrowing  family  is  not  left  in
wealthy circumstances.    Most certainly it is pity when
a generous emotion, in many men, or in any man, has
to die out futile, and leave no *action* behind it.    The
question, therefore, suggests itself—Should not there
be  a  'Braidwood  Testimonial,'  the  proper  parties
undertaking it, in a modest, serious manner, the public
silently testifying (to such extent, at least) what worth
its emotion has ?

" I venture to throw out this hint, and, if it be acted
on, will, with great satisfaction, give my mite among
other people ; but must, for good reasons, say further,
that this [is] all I can do in the  matter (of which, indeed, I know nothing but what everybody knows, and
a great deal less than every reader of the newspapers
knows) ; and that, in particular, I cannot answer any
letters on the subject, should such happen to be sent
me.

" In haste, I remain, Sir, your obedient servant,

" T. CARLYLE.*

" 5, Cheyne-row, Chelsea, June 30."

* (Printed in *The Times*, Tuesday, July 2, 1861.)

The "History of Frederick the Great" was completed early in 1865. Later in the same year the students of Edinburgh University elected Carlyle as Lord Rector. We cannot do better than describe the proceedings and the subsequent address in the words of the late Alexander Smith :—

"Mr. Gladstone demitted office, and then it behoved the students of the University to cast about for a worthy successor. Two candidates were proposed, Mr. Carlyle and Mr. Disraeli; and on the election day Mr. Carlyle was returned by a large and enthusiastic majority. This was all very well, but a doubt lingered in the minds of many whether Mr. Carlyle would accept the office, or if accepting it, whether he would deliver an address—said address being the sole apple which the Rectorial tree is capable of bearing. The hare was indeed caught, but it was doubtful somewhat whether the hare would allow itself to be *cooked* after the approved academical fashion. It was tolerably well known that Mr. Carlyle had emerged from his long spell of work on " Frederick," in a condition of health the reverse of robust; that he had once or twice before declined similar honours from Scottish Universities—from Glasgow some twelve or fourteen years ago, and from Aberdeen some seven or eight; and that he was constitutionally opposed to all varieties of popular displays, more especially those of the oratorical sort.

"But all dispute was ended when it was officially announced that Mr. Carlyle had accepted the office of Lord Rector, that he would conform to all its requirements, and that the Rectorial address would be delivered late in spring. And so when the days began to lengthen in these northern latitudes, and crocuses to show their yellow and purple heads, people began to talk about the visit of the great writer, and to speculate on what manner and fashion of speech he would deliver.

"Edinburgh has no University Hall, and accordingly when speech-day approached, the largest public room in the city was chartered by the University authorities. This public room—the Music Hall in George Street—will contain, under severe pressure, from eighteen hundred to nineteen hundred persons, and tickets to that extent were secured by the students and members of the General Council. Curious stories are told of the eagerness on every side manifested to hear Mr. Carlyle. Country clergymen from beyond Aberdeen

came into Edinburgh for the sole purpose of hearing
and seeing.  Gentlemen came down from London by
train the night before, and returned to London by
train the night after.

 " In a very few minutes after the doors were opened
the large hall was filled in every part, and when up
the central passage the Principal, the Lord Rector, the
Members of the Senate, and other gentlemen advanced
towards the platform, the cheering was vociferous and
hearty.  The Principal occupied the chair of course,
the Lord Rector on his right, the Lord Provost on his
left.  Every eye was fixed on the Rector.  To all appearance, as he sat, time and labour had dealt tenderly
with him.  His face had not yet lost the country
bronze which he brought up with him from Dumfriesshire as a student fifty-six years ago.  His long residence in London had not touched his Annandale
look, nor had it—as we soon learned—touched his
Annandale accent.  His countenance was striking,
homely, sincere, truthful—the countenance of a man
on whom ' the burden of the unintelligible world ' had
weighed more heavily than on most.  His hair was
yet almost dark ; his moustache and short beard were
iron grey.  His eyes were wide, melancholy, sorrowful;

and seemed as if they had been at times a-weary of the sun. Altogether in his aspect there was something aboriginal, as of a piece of unhewn granite, which had never been polished to any approved pattern, whose natural and original vitality had never been tampered with. In a word, there seemed no passivity about Mr. Carlyle—he was the diamond, and the world was his pane of glass; he was a graving tool rather than a thing graven upon—a man to set his mark on the world—a man on whom the world could not set *its* mark. And just as, glancing towards Fife a few minutes before, one could not help thinking of his early connection with Edward Irving, so seeing him sit beside the venerable Principal of the University, one could not help thinking of his earliest connection with literature.

" Time brings men into the most unexpected relationships. When the Principal was plain Mr. Brewster, editor of the Edinburgh Cyclopædia, little dreaming that he should ever be Knight of Hanover and head of the Northern Metropolitan University, Mr. Carlyle—just as little dreaming that he should be the foremost man of letters of his day and Lord Rector of the same University—was his contributor, writing for said Cyclopædia biographies of Montesquieu and other notables. And so it came about that after years of separation and of honourable labour, the old editor and contributor were brought together again—in new aspects.

"The proceedings began by the conferring of the degree of LL.D. on Mr. Erskine of Linlathen—an old friend of Mr. Carlyle's—on Professors Huxley, Tyndall, and Ramsay, and on Dr. Rae, the Arctic explorer. That done, amid a tempest of cheering and hats enthusiastically waved, Mr. Carlyle, slipping off his Rectorial robe—which must have been a very shirt of Nessus to him—advanced to the table and began to speak in low, wavering, melancholy tones, which were in accordance with the melancholy eyes, and in the Annandale accent, with which his playfellows must have been familiar long ago. So self-contained was he, so impregnable to outward influences, that all his years of Edinburgh and London life could not impair even in the slightest degree, *that.*

"The opening sentences were lost in the applause. What need of quoting a speech which by this time has been read by everybody? Appraise it as you please, it was a thing *per se.* Just as, if you wish a purple dye you must fish up the Murex; if you wish ivory you must go to the east; so if you desire an address such as Edinburgh listened to the other day, you must go to Chelsea for it. It may not be quite to your taste, but, in any case, there is no other intellectual warehouse in which that kind of article is kept in stock.

"The gratitude I owe to him is—or should be—equal to that of most. He has been to me only a voice, sometimes sad, sometimes wrathful, sometimes scornful; and when I saw him for the first time with the eye of flesh stand up amongst us the other day, and heard him speak kindly, brotherly, affectionate words—his first appearance of that kind, I suppose, since he discoursed of Heroes and Hero Worship to the London people—I am not ashamed to confess that I felt moved towards him, as I do not think in any possible combination of circumstances I could have felt moved towards any other living-man."*

The Edinburgh correspondent to a London paper thus describes what took place :—

"A vast interest among the intelligent public has

* *The Argosy,* May, 1866.

been excited by the prospect of Mr. Thomas Carlyle's appearance to be installed as Lord Rector of the University of Edinburgh. With the exception of the delivery of his lectures on Heroes and Hero-worship, he has avoided oratory; and to many of his admirers the present occasion seemed likely to afford their only chance of ever seeing him in the flesh, and hearing his living voice. The result has been, that the University authorities have been beset by applications in number altogether unprecedented—to nearly all of which they could only give the reluctant answer, that admission for strangers was impossible. The students who elect Mr. Carlyle received tickets, if they applied within the specified time, and the members of the University council, or graduates, obtained the residue according to priority of application. Ladies' tickets to the number of one hundred and fifty were issued, each professor obtaining four, and the remaining thirty being placed at the disposal of Sir David Brewster, the Principal. And the one hundred and fifty lucky ladies were conspicuous in the front of the gallery to-day, having been admitted before the doors for students and other males were open.

"The hour appointed for letting them in was kept

**6**

precisely—it was half-past one P.M., but an hour before it, despite occasional showers of rain, a crowd had begun to gather at the front door of the music-hall, and at the opening of the door it had gathered to proportions sufficient to half fill the building, its capacity under severe crushing being about two thousand.

"When the door was opened, they rushed in as crowds of young men only can and dare rush, and up the double stairs they streamed like a torrent; which torrent, however, policemen and check-gates soon moderated. I chanced to fall into a lucky current of the crowd, and got in amongst the first two or three hundred, and got forward to the fourth seat from the platform, as good a place for seeing and hearing as any.

"The proceedings of the day were fixed to commence at two P.M., and the half-hour of waiting was filled up by the students in throwing occasional volleys of peas, whistling *en masse* various lively tunes, and in clambering, like small escalading parties, on to and over the platform to take advantage of the seats in the organ gallery behind. For Edinburgh students, however, let me say that these proceedings were singularly decorous. They did indulge in a little fun when nothing else was doing, but they did not come for that alone. Any student who wanted fun could have sold his ticket at a handsome profit, for which better fun could be had elsewhere. I heard among the crowd that some students had got so high a price as a guinea each for their tickets, and I heard of others who had been offered no less but had refused it. And I must say further, that they listened to Mr. Carlyle's address with as much attention and reverence as they could have bestowed on a prophet— only I daresay most prophets would have elicited less applause and laughter.

"Shortly before two, the city magistrates and a few other personages mounted the platform, and, with as much quietness as the fancy of the students directed, took the seats which had been marked out for them by large red pasteboard tickets. At two precisely the students in the organ gallery started to the tops of the seats and began to cheer vociferously, and almost instantly all the audience followed their example. The procession was on its way through the hall, and in half a minute Lord Provost Chambers, in his official robes, mounted the platform stair; then Principal

Sir David Brewster and Lord Rector Carlyle, both in
their gold-laced robes of office; then the Rev. Dr.
Lee, and the other professors, in their gowns; also
the LL.D.'s to be, in black gowns.    Lord Neaves and
Dr. Guthrie were there in an LL.D.'s black gown and
blue ribbons; Mr. Harvey, the President of the
Royal Academy, and Sir D. Baxter, Bart.—men con
spicuous in their plain clothes.

" Dr. Lee offered up a prayer of a minute and a
half, at the ' Amen ' of which I could see Mr. Carlyle bow very low.    Then the business of the occasior
commenced.    Mr. Gibson—a tall, thin, pale-faced,
beardless, acute, composed-looking young gentleman,
in an M.A.'s gown—introduced Mr. Carlyle, ' the
most distinguished son of the University,' to the
Principal, Sir David Brewster, as the Lord Rector
elected by the students.    Sir David saluted him as
such, thinking, perhaps, of the time when, an unknown young man, Thomas Carlyle wrote articles for
Brewster's ' Cyclopædia,' and got Brewster's name to
introduce to public notice his translation of Legendre's ' Geometry.'    Next Professor Muirhead, for the
time being the Dean of the Faculty of Laws in the
University, introduced various gentlemen to the Prin-

cipal in order, as persons whom the senate had thought worthy of the degree of LL.D., giving a dignified, but not always very happy, account of the merits of each.   There was Mr. Erskine, of Linlathen, Mr. Carlyle's host for the time being, and often previously, an old friend of Irving and Chalmers, himself the writer of various elegant and sincere religious books, and one of the best and most amiable of men. If intelligent goodness ever entitled any one to the degree of LL.D., he certainly deserves it ; and when I say this, I do not insinuate that on grounds of pure intellect he is not well entitled to the honour.   He is now, I should think, nearer eighty than seventy years of age—a mild-looking, full-eyed old man, with a face somewhat of the type of Lord Derby's.   There was Professor Huxley, young in years, dark, heavy-browed, alert and resolute, but not moulded after any high ideal ; and there was Professor Tyndal, also young, lithe of limb, and nonchalant in manner.   When his name was called he sat as if he had no concern in what was going on, and then rose with an easy smile, partly of modesty, but in great measure of indifference.

"Dr. Rae, the Arctic explorer and first discoverer

of the fate of Sir John Franklin, who is an M.D. of
Edinburgh, was now made LL.D. He is of tall, wiry,
energetic figure, slightly baldish, with greyish, curly
hair, keen, handsome face, high crown and sloping
forehead, and his bearing is that of a soldier—of a
man who has both given and obeyed commands, and
been drilled to stand steady and upright. Carlyle
himself was offered the degree of LL.D., but he declined the honour, laughing it off, in fact, in a letter,
with such excuses as that he had a brother a Dr.
Carlyle (an M.D., also a man of genius, I insert
parenthetically, and known in literature as a translator
of ' Dante'), and that if two Dr. Carlyles should appear at Paradise, mistakes might arise.

" After all the LL.D.s had heard their merits enu-
merated, and had had a black hood or wallet of some
kind, with a blue ribbon conspicuous in it, flung over
their heads, Principal Brewster announced that the
Lord Rector would now deliver his address. There-
upon Mr. Carlyle rose at once, shook himself out of
his gold-laced rectorial gown, left it on his chair, and
stepped quietly to the table, and drawing his tall,
bony frame into a position of straight perpendicu-
larity not possible to one man in five hundred at

seventy years of age, he began to speak quietly and
distinctly, but nervously.   There was a slight flush on
his face, but he bore himself with composure and
dignity, and in the course of half an hour he was
obviously beginning to feel at his ease, so far at least
as to have adequate command over the current of his
thought.

"He spoke on quite freely and easily, hardly ever
repeated a word, never looked at a note, and only
once returned to finish up a topic from which he had
deviated.   He apologised for not having come with a
written discourse.   It was usual, and 'it would have
been more comfortable for me just at present,' but he
had tried it, and could not satisfy himself, and 'as the
spoken word comes from the heart,' he had resolved
to try that method.   What he said in words will be
learned otherwise than from me.   I could not well
describe it; but I do not think I ever heard any address that I should be so unwilling to blot from my
memory.   Not that there was much in it that cannot
be found in his writings, or inferred from them; but the
manner of the man was a key to the writings, and for
naturalness and quiet power, I have never seen anything to compare with it.   He did not deal in rhe-

toric. He talked—it was continuous, strong, quiet talk—like a patriarch about to leave the world to the young lads who had chosen him and were just entering the world. His voice is a soft, downy voice— not a tone in it is of the shrill, fierce kind that one would expect it to be in reading the Latter-day Pamphlets.

"There was not a trace of effort or of affectation, or even of extravagance. Shrewd common sense there was in abundance. There was the involved disrupted style also, but it looked so natural that reflection was needed to recognise in it that very style which purists find to be un-English and unintelligible. Over the angles of this disrupted style rolled out a few cascades of humour—quite as if by accident. He let them go, talking on in his soft, downy accents, without a smile; occasionally for an instant looking very serious, with his dark eyes beating like pulses, but generally looking merely composed and kindly, and so, to speak, father-like. He concluded by reciting his own translation of a poem of Goethe—

"'The future hides in it gladness and sorrow.'

And this he did in a style of melancholy grandeur not

to be described, but still l ss to be forgotten.    It was
then alone that the personality of the philosopher
and poet were revealed continuously in his manner of
utterance.    The features of his face are familiar to all
from his portraits.    But I do not think any portrait,
unless, perhaps, Woolner's medallion, gives full expression to the resolution that is visible in his face.
Besides, they all make him look sadder and older
than he appears.    Although he be threescore and ten,
his hair is still abundant and tolerably black, and
there is considerable colour in his cheek.    Not a man
of his age on that platform to-day looked so young,
and he had done more work than any ten on it."

The correspondent of the *Pall Mall Gazette* gives
some interesting particulars :—

" Mr. Carlyle had not spoken in public before yesterday, since those grand utterances on Heroes and
Hero-worship in the institute in Edwards Street,
Marylebone, which one can scarcely believe, whilst
reading them, to have been, in the best sense, extemporaneously delivered.    In that case Mr. Carlyle
began the series, as we have heard, by bringing a

manuscript which he evidently found much in his way, and presently abandoned. On the second evening he brought some notes or headings; but these also tripped him until he had left them. The remaining lectures were given like his conversation, which no one can hear without feeling that, with all its glow and inspiration, every sentence would be, if taken down, found faultless. It was so in his remarkable extemporaneous address yesterday. He had no notes whatever. 'But,' says our correspondent, in transmitting the report, 'I have never heard a speech of whose more remarkable qualities so few can be conveyed on paper. You will read of "applause" and "laughter," but you will little realize the eloquent blood flaming up the speaker's cheek, the kindling of his eye, or the inexpressible voice and look when the drolleries were coming out. When he spoke of clap-trap books exciting astonishment 'in the minds of foolish persons,' the evident halting at the word '*fools*,' and the smoothing of his hair, as if he must be decorous, which preceded the change to 'foolish persons,' were exceedingly comical. As for the flaming bursts, they took shape in grand tones, whose impression was made deeper, not by raising, but by lowering the voice.

Your correspondent here declares that he should hold it worth his coming all the way from London in the rain in the Sunday night train were it only to have heard Carlyle say, " There is a nobler ambition than the gaining of all California, or the getting of all the suffrages that are on the planet just now !"' In the first few minutes of the address there was some hesitation, and much of the shrinking that one might expect in a secluded scholar ; but these very soon cleared away, and during the larger part, and to the close of the oration, it was evident that he was receiving a sympathetic influence from his listeners, which he did not fail to return tenfold. The applause became less frequent ; the silence became that of a woven spell ; and the recitation of the beautiful lines from Goethe, at the end, was so masterly—so marvellous—that one felt in it that Carlyle's real anathemas against rhetoric were but the expression of his knowledge that there is a rhetoric beyond all other arts."

In the *Times* the following leader appeared upon Mr. Carlyle's address :—

" There is something in the return of a man to the

haunts of his youth, after he has acquired fame and
a recognised position in the world, which is of itself
sufficient to arrest attention.   We are interested in the
retrospect and the contrast, the juxtaposition of the
old and the new, the hopes of early years, the memory
of the struggles and contests of manhood, the repose
of victory.   A man may differ as much as he pleases
from the doctrines of Mr. Carlyle, he may reject his
historical teachings, and may distrust his politics, but
he must be of a very unkindly disposition not to be
touched by his reception at Edinburgh.   It is fifty-four
years, he told the students of the University, since he,
a boy of fourteen, came as a student, 'full of wonder
and expectation,' to the old capital of his native
country, and now he returns, having accomplished the
days of man spoken of by the Psalmist, that he may
be honoured by students of this generation, and may
give them a few words of advice on the life which lies
before them.

"The discourse of the new Lord Rector squared
very well with the occasion.   There was no novelty
in it.   New truths are not the gifts which the old offer
the young; the lesson we learn last is but the fulness
of the meaning of what was only partially apprehended

at first.    Mr. Carlyle brought out things familiar
enough to everyone who has read his works; there
were the old platitudes and the old truths, and, it
must be owned, mingled here and there with them the
old errors.    Time has, however, its recompenses, and
if the freshness of youth seemed to be wanting in the
address of the Rector, so also was its crudity.    There
was a singular mellowness in Mr. Carlyle's speech,
which was reflected in the homely language in which
it was couched.    The chief lessons he had to enforce
were to avoid cram, and to be painstaking, diligent,
and patient in the acquisition of knowledge.    Students
are not to try to make themselves acquainted with the
outsides of as many things as possible, and 'to go
flourishing about' upon the strength of their acquisi-
tions, but to count a thing as known only when it is
stamped on their mind.    The doctrine is only a new
reading of the old maxim, *non multa sed multum*, but
it is as much needed now as ever it was.    Still more
appropriate to the present day was Mr. Carlyle's pro-
test against the notion that a University is the place
where a man is to be fitted for the special work of a
profession.    A University, as he puts it, teaches a
man how to read, or, as we may say more generally,

how to learn. It is not the function of such a place to offer particular and technical knowledge, but to prepare a man for mastering any science by teaching him the method of all. A child learns the use of his body, not the art of a carpenter or smith, and the University student learns the use of his mind, not the professional lore of a lawyer or a physician. It is pleasant to meet with a strong reassertion of doctrines which the utilitarianism of a commercial and manufacturing age is too apt to make us all forget. Mr. Carlyle is essentially conservative in his notions on academic functions. Accuracy, discrimination, judgment, are with him the be-all and end-all of educational training. If a man has learnt to know a thing in itself, and in its relation to surrounding phenomena, he has got from a University what it is its proper duty to teach. Accordingly, we find him bestowing a good word on poor old Arthur Collins, who showed that he possessed these valuable qualities in the humble work of compiling a Peerage.

" The new Lord Rector is, however, as conservative in his choice of the implements of study as he is in the determination of its objects. The languages and the history of the great nations of antiquity he puts foremost, like any other pedagogue. The Greeks and the Romans are, he tells the Edinburgh students, 'a pair of nations shining in the records left by themselves as a kind of pillar to light up life in the darkness of the past ages;' and he adds that it would be well worth their while to get an understanding of what these people were, and what they did. It is here, however, that an old error of Mr. Carlyle's crops up among his well-remembered truths. He quotes from Machiavelli—evidently agreeing himself with the sentiment, though he refrained from asking the assent of his audience to it—the statement that the history of Rome showed that a democracy could not permanently exist without the occasional intervention of a Dictator. It is possible that if Machiavelli had had the experience of the centuries which have elapsed since his day, he would have seen fit to alter his conclusion, and it is to be regretted that the admiration which Mr. Carlyle ·feels for the great men of history will not allow him to believe in the possibility of a political society where each might find his proper sphere and duty without disturbing the order and natural succession of the commonwealth. His judgment on this point is like that of a man who had only known the

steam-engine before the invention of governor balls,
and was ready to declare that its mechanism would be
shattered if a boy were not always at hand to regulate
the pressure of the steam.

*        *        *        *        *

"We may turn, however, from this difference to
another of Mr. Carlyle's doctrines, which mark at
once his independence of thought and his respect for
experience, where he declares the necessity for recog-
nising the hereditary principle in government, if there
is to be 'any fixity in things.' In the same way
we find him almost lamenting the fact that Oxford,
once apparently so fast-anchored as to be immov-
able, has begun to twist and toss on the eddy of new
ideas.

"It is impossible to glance at Mr. Carlyle's Easter
Monday discourse without recalling the oration which
his predecessor pronounced on resigning office last
autumn. * * * Mr. Carlyle is as simple and practical
as his predecessor was dazzling and rhetorical. An
ounce of mother wit, quotes the new Lord Rector, is
worth a pound of clergy, and while he admires Demosthenes, he prefers the eloquence of Phocion. A
little later he repeats his old doctrine on the virtue of

silence, laments the fact that 'the finest nations in the world—the English and the American—are going all away into wind and tongue,' and protests that a man is not to be esteemed wise because he has poured out speech copiously.   Mr. Carlyle has so often inculcated these sentiments in his books that there can be no suspicion of an *arrière pensée* in their utterance · now, but the contrast between him and his predecessor is at the least instructive.   Each does, however, in some measure, supply what is deficient in the other. No one would claim for the Chancellor of the Exchequer the intensity of power of his successor, but in his abundant energy, his wide sympathy with popular movement, and his real, if vague and indiscriminating, faith in the activity and progress of modern life, he conveys lessons of trust in the present, and hopefulness in the future, which would be ill-exchanged for the patient and somewhat sad stoicism of Mr. Carlyle."

Carlyle was still in Scotland on April 21, and there the terrible and solemn news had to be conveyed to him of the sudden death of her who had been his true and faithful life-companion for forty years.

Mrs. Carlyle died on Saturday, April 21, under

very peculiar circumstances. She was taking her usual drive in Hyde Park about four o'clock, when her little favourite dog—which was running by the side of the brougham—was run over by a carriage. She was greatly alarmed, though the dog was not seriously hurt. She lifted the dog into the carriage, and the man drove on. Not receiving any call or direction from his mistress, as was usual, he stopped the carriage and discovered her, as he thought, in a fit, or ill, and drove to St. George's Hospital, which was near at hand. When there it was discovered that she must have been dead some little time. Mrs. Carlyle's health had been for several months feeble, but not in a state to excite anxiety or alarm.

On the following Wednesday her remains were conveyed from London to Haddington for interment there, and the funeral took place on Thursday afternoon. Mr. Carlyle was accompanied from London (whither he had returned immediately on the receipt of that solemn message) by his brother, Dr. Carlyle, Mr. John Forster, and the Hon. Mr. Twistleton. The funeral cortège consisted of a hearse and two carriages, and was followed on foot by a large number of gentlemen who had known Mrs. Carlyle and her father, Dr. Welsh, who was held in high estimation in the town, where he had practised medicine till his death, in 1819. The grave, which is the same as that occupied by Dr. Welsh, lies in the centre of the ruined choir of the old cathedral at Haddington *  * In accordance with the Scottish practice, there was no service read, and Mr. Carlyle threw a handful of earth on the coffin after it had been lowered into the grave.

Carlyle wrote the following inscription to be placed on his wife's tombstone :—

" Here likewise now rests Jane Welsh Carlyle, spouse of Thomas Carlyle, Chelsea, London. She was born at Hadding-ton 14th July, 1801; only child of the above John Welsh and of Grace Welsh, Caplegell, Dumfriesshire, his wife. In her bright existence she had more sorrows than are common, but also a soft invincibility, a capacity of discernment, and a noble loyalty of heart which are rare. For 40 years she was the true and loving helpmate of her husband, and by act and word unweariedly forwarded him as none else could in all of worthy that he did or attempted. She died at London, 21st April, 1866, suddenly snatched away from him, and the light of his life as if gone out."

Later in the same year, weighed down as he was by his great sorrow, Carlyle nevertheless thought it a public duty to come forward in defence of Governor

Eyre, and raise his voice against the persecution of
that faithful public servant.   He acted as Vice-President
of the Defence Fund.   The following is a letter
written to Mr. Hamilton Hume, giving his views on
the subject in full :

"Ripple Court, Ringwould, Dover,
"*August* 23, 1866.

"SIR,

"The clamour raised against Governor Eyre
appears to me to be disgraceful to the good sense of
England ; and if it rested on any depth of conviction,
and were not rather (as I always flatter myself it is) a
thing of rumour and hearsay, of repetition and rever-
beration, mostly from the teeth outward, I should
consider it of evil omen to the country and to its
highest interests in these times.   For my own share,
all the light that has yet reached me on Mr. Eyre and
his history in the world goes steadily to establish the
conclusion that he is a just, humane, and valiant man,
faithful to his trusts everywhere, and with no ordinary
faculty of executing them; that his late services in
Jamaica were of great, perhaps of incalculable value,
as certainly they were of perilous and appalling diffi-

culty—something like the case of 'fire,' suddenly reported, 'in the ship's powder room,' in mid-ocean, where the moments mean the ages, and life and death hang on your use or misuse of the moments; and, in short, that penalty and clamour are not the thing this Governor merits from any of us, but honour and thanks, and wise imitation (I will farther say), should similar emergencies arise, on the great scale or on the small, in whatever we are governing!

"The English nation never loved anarchy, nor was wont to spend its sympathy on miserable mad seditions, especially of this inhuman and half-brutish type; but always loved order, and the prompt suppression of seditions, and reserved its tears for something worthier than promoters of such delirious and fatal enterprises who had got their wages for their sad industry. Has the English nation changed, then, altogether? I flatter myself it is not, not yet quite; but only that certain loose, superficial portions of it have become a great deal louder, and not any wiser, than they formerly used to be.

"At any rate, though much averse, at any time, and at this time in particular, to figure on committees, or run into public noises without call, I do at once, and

feel that as a British citizen I should, and must, make
you welcome to my name for your committee, and to
whatever good it can do you. With the hope only
that many other British men, of far more significance
in such a matter, will at once or gradually do the like;
and that, in fine, by wise effort and persistence, a
blind and disgraceful act of public injustice may be
prevented; and an egregrious folly as well—not to
say, for none can say or compute, what a vital detriment throughout the British Empire, in such an example set to all the colonies and governors the British
Empire has!

"Farther service, I fear, I am not in a state to promise, but the whole weight of my conviction and good
wishes is with you; and if other service possible to
me do present itself, I shall not want for willingness in
case of need. Enclosed is my mite of contribution to
your fund.

"I have the honour to be yours truly,

"T. CARLYLE."

"To HAMILTON HUME, Esq.,
"Hon. Sec. 'Eyre Defence Fund.'"


With respect to the portraits of Carlyle, one of

the first, if not the earliest, was a full length sketch published in Fraser's Magazine in June 1833, when he was in his thirty-eight year.    Another taken by Samuel Lawrence, about 1843, is perhaps the most intellectual-looking of all the published likenesses; the beetle-browed, stern figure presents to one's mind the very ideal of a giant in thought.    Count D'Orsay's sketch, published by Mitchell in 1839, is highly characteristic of the artist, and if Carlyle should ever relax his opinions upon society, and desire to go down to posterity as a fashionable personage, rather than as a stern moralist, this will be his favourite portrait.    It was taken when no man of position was counted a dutiful subject who did not wear a black satin stock and a Petersham coat.    The portrait on our cover is from a sketch by a friend, taken in 1859.    It is an admirable likeness.    Another by Maclise may be seen in the large cartoon etching of the writers in Fraser's Magazine, 1835.    It represents a banquet—one of those given by Maginn and Fraser—in the snug room at the back of the shop, 212, Regent Street.    Maginn is in the chair, and around the table may be seen Barry Cornwall, Southey, Thackeray, Macnish, Ainsworth, Coleridge, Hogg, Croker, Lockhart, Theodore

Hook, Sir David Brewster, D'Orsay, Carlyle, and many others.

An excellent portrait appeared some time ago in the *Illustrated London News*, and another, not quite so good, came out in the now defunct *Critic*, in 1859. The medallion by Woolner is very artistic, but scarcely conveys the peculiarities of the face. Recently some admirable photographs have appeared, but they are too true—painfully true—for, with the peculiarity of the lens, the wrinkles and seams in the face are intensified in such a manner as to give an unnatural, if not unhealthy expression. If we are mortal, we need not always be looked at through an optical glass.

The following anecdotes of Carlyle are told by Mr. Lewes in his " Life of Goethe " :—

" I heard a capital story of Carlyle at a dinner-party in Berlin, silencing the cant about Goethe's want of religion, by one of his characteristic sarcasms. For some time he sat quiet, but not patient, while certain pietists were throwing up their eyes, and regretting that so great a genius ! so godlike a genius ! should not have more purely devoted himself to the service of Christian truth ! and should have had so little, etc., etc.  Carlyle sat grim, ominously silent, his hands impatiently twisting his napkin, until at last he broke silence, and in his slow, emphatic way said, ' Meine Herren, did you never hear the story of that man who vilified the sun because it would not light his cigar ?'  This bombshell completely silenced the enemy's fire." *

" I remember once, as we were walking along Piccadilly, talking about the infamous *Buchlein von Goethe*, Carlyle stopped suddenly, and with his peculiar look and emphasis, said, ' Yes, it is the wild cry of amazement on the part of all spooneys that the Titan was not a spooney too !  Here is a godlike intellect, and yet you see he is not an idiot !  Not in the least a spooney !' " †

* From "The Life of Goethe," by George Henry Lewes. Second Edition, 1864, p. 521.

† *Ib.*, p. 256.

# ADDRESS

DELIVERED TO THE

## STUDENTS OF THE UNIVERSITY OF EDINBURGH

### APRIL 2, 1866.

GENTLEMEN,

I HAVE accepted the office you have elected me to, and have now the duty to return thanks for the great honour done me. Your enthusiasm towards me, I admit, is very beautiful in itself, however undesirable it may be in regard to the object of it. It is a feeling honourable to all men, and one well known to myself when I was in a position analogous to your own. I can only hope that it may endure to the end—

that noble desire to honour those whom you think worthy of honour, and come to be more and more select and discriminate in the choice of the object of it ; for I can well understand that you will modify your opinions of me and many things else as you go on. (Laughter and cheers.)   There are now fifty-six years gone last November since I first entered your city, a boy of not quite fourteen—fifty-six years ago—to attend classes here and gain knowledge of all kinds, I know not what, with feelings of wonder and awe-struck expectation ; and now, after a long, long course, this is what we have come to. (Cheers.)   There is something touching and tragic, and yet at the same time beautiful, to see the third generation, as it were, of my dear old native land, rising up and saying, " Well, you are not altogether an unworthy labourer in the vineyard : you have toiled through a great variety of fortunes, and have had many judges." As the old proverb says, " He that builds by the wayside has many masters." We must expect a variety of judges; but the voice of young Scotland, through you, is really of some value to me, and I return you many thanks for it, though. I cannot describe my emotions to you, and perhaps they will be much more conceivable if expressed in silence. (Cheers.)

When this office was proposed to me, some of you know that I was not very ambitious to accept it, at first. I was taught to believe that there were more or less certain important duties which would lie in my power. This, I confess, was my chief motive in going into it— at least, in reconciling the objections felt to such things; for if I can do anything to honour you and my dear old *Alma Mater*, why should I not do so? (Loud cheers.) Well, but on practically looking into the matter when the office actually came into my hands, I find it grows more and more uncertain and abstruse to me whether there is much real duty that I can do at all.   I live four hundred miles away from you, in an entirely different state of things ; and my weak health—now for many years accumulating upon me—and a total unacquaintance with such subjects as concern your affairs here,—all this fills me with apprehension that there is really nothing worth the least consideration that I can do on that score.   You may, however, depend upon it that if any such duty does arise in any form, I will use my most faithful endeavour to do whatever is right and proper, according to the best of my judgment.   (Cheers.)

In the meanwhile, the duty I have at present —which might be very pleasant, but which is quite the reverse, as you may fancy—is to address some words to you on some subjects more or less cognate to the pursuits you are engaged in.   In fact, I had meant to throw out some loose observations—loose in point of order, I mean—in such a way as they may occur to me —the truths I have in me about the business you are engaged in, the race you have started on, what kind of race it is you young gentlemen have begun, and what sort of arena you are likely to find in this world. I ought, I believe, according to custom, to have written all that down on paper, and had it read out. That would have been much handier for me at the present moment (a laugh), but when I attempted to write, I found that I was not accustomed to write speeches, and that I did not get on very well. So I flung that away, and resolved to trust to the inspiration of the moment—just to what came uppermost. You will therefore have to accept what is readiest, what comes direct from the heart, and you must just take that in compensation for any good order of arrangement there might have been in it.

I will endeavour to say nothing that is not true, as far as I can manage, and that is pretty much all that I can engage for. (A laugh.) Advices, I believe, to young men—and to all

men—are very seldom much valued. There is
a great deal of advising, and very little faithful
performing. And talk that does not end in any
kind of action, is better suppressed altogether.
I would ·not, therefore, go much into advising ;
but there is one advice I must give you. It is,
in fact, the summary of all advices, and you
have heard it a thousand times, I dare say ; but
I must, nevertheless, let you hear it the thousand
and first time, for it is most intensely true,
whether you will believe it at present or not—
namely, that above all things the interest of your
own life depends upon being diligent now, while
it is called to-day, in this place where you have
come to get education. Diligent! That includes
all virtues in it that a student can have ; I mean
to include in it all qualities that lead into the
acquirement of real instruction and improvement
in such a place. If you will believe me, you
who are young, yours is the golden season of
life. As you have heard it called, so it verily is,

the seed-time of life, in which, if you do not
sow, or if you sow tares instead of wheat, you
cannot expect to reap well afterwards, and you
will arrive at indeed little; while in the course of
years, when you come to look back, and if you
have not done what you have heard from your
advisers—and among many counsellers there is
wisdom—you will bitterly repent when it is too
late. The habits of study acquired at Universities are of the highest importance in after-life.
At the season when you are in young years the
whole mind is, as it were, fluid, and is capable of
forming itself into any shape that the owner of
the mind pleases to order it to form itself into.
The mind is in a fluid state, but it hardens up
gradually to the consistency of rock or iron, and
you cannot alter the habits of an old man, but as
he has begun he will proceed and go on to the
last. By diligence, I mean among other things
—and very chiefly—honesty in all your inquiries
into what you are about. Pursue your studies

8

in the way your conscience calls honest. More
and more endeavour to do that. Keep, I mean
to say, an accurate separation of what you have
really come to know in your own minds, and
what is still unknown. Leave all that on the
hypothetical side of the barrier, as things
afterwards to be acquired, if acquired at all ;
and be careful not to stamp a thing as known
when you do not yet know it. Count a thing
known only when it is stamped on your mind,
so that you may survey it on all sides with in-
telligence.

There is such a thing as a man endeavouring
to persuade himself, and endeavouring to persuade others, that he knows about things when
he does not know more than the outside skin of
them ; and he goes flourishing about with them.
("Hear, hear," and a laugh.) There is also a
process called cramming in some Universities
(a laugh)—that is, getting up such points of
things as the examiner is likely to put questions

about.  Avoid all that as entirely unworthy of
an honourable habit.  Be modest, and humble,
and diligent in your attention to what your
teachers tell you, who are profoundly interested
in trying to bring you forward in the right way,
so far as they have been able to understand it.
Try all things they set before you, in order, if
possible, to understand them, and to value them
in proportion to your fitness for them.  Gradually see what kind of work you can do ; for it is
the first of all problems for a man to find out
what kind of work he is to do in this universe.
In fact, morality as regards study is, as in all
other things, the primary consideration, and
overrides all others.  A dishonest man cannot
do anything real ; and it would be greatly better
if he were tied up from doing any such thing.
He does nothing but darken counsel by the
words he utters.  That is a very old doctrine,
but a very true one ; and you will find it con-
firmed by all the thinking men that have ever

lived in this long series of generations of which we are the latest.

I daresay you know, very many of you, that it is now seven hundred years since Universities were first set up in this world of ours. Abelard and other people had risen up with doctrines in them the people wished to hear of, and students flocked towards them from all parts of the world. There was no getting the thing recorded in books as you may now. You had to hear him speaking to you vocally, or else you could not learn at all what it was that he wanted to say. And so they gathered together the various people who had anything to teach, and formed themselves gradually, under the patronage of kings and other potentates who were anxious about the culture of their populations, nobly anxious for their benefit, and became a University.

I daresay, perhaps, you have heard it said that all that is greatly altered by the invention

of printing, which took place about midway between us and the origin of Universities.. A man
has not now to go away to where a professor is
actually speaking, because in most cases he can
get his doctrine out of him through a book, and
can read it, and read it again and again, and
study it. I don't know that I know of any way
in which the whole facts of a subject may be
more completely taken in, if our studies are
moulded in conformity with it. Nevertheless,
Universities have, and will continue to have, an
indispensable value in society — a very high
value. I consider the very highest interests of
man vitally intrusted to them.

In regard to theology, as you are aware, it has
been the study of the deepest heads that have
come into the world—what is the nature of this
stupendous universe, and what its relations to all
things, as known to man, and as only known to
the awful Author of it. In fact, the members
of the Church keep theology in a lively con-

dition (laughter), for the benefit of the whole population, which is the great object of our Universities. I consider it is the same now intrinsically, though very much forgotten, from many causes, and not so successful as might be wished at all. (A laugh.) It remains, however, a very curious truth, what has been said by observant people, that the main use of the Universities in the present age is that, after you have done with all your classes, the next thing is a collection of books, a great library of good books, which you proceed to study and to read. What the Universities have mainly done—what I have found the University did for me, was that it taught me to read in various languages and various sciences, so that I could go into the books that treated of these things, and try anything I wanted to make myself master of gradually, as I found it suit me. Whatever you may think of all that, the clearest and most imperative duty lies on every one of you to be assiduous in your reading ; and learn to be good readers, which is, perhaps, a more difficult thing than you imagine. Learn to be discriminative in your reading—to read all kinds of things that you have an interest in, and that you find to be really fit for what you are engaged in. Of course, at the present time, in a great deal of the reading incumbent on you you must be guided by the books recommended to you by your professors for assistance towards the prelections. And then, when you get out of the University, and go into studies of your own, you will find it very important that you have selected a field, a province in which you can study and work.

The most unhappy of all men is the man that cannot tell what he is going to do, that has got no work cut out for him in the world, and does not go into it. For work is the grand cure of all the maladies and miseries that ever beset mankind—honest work, which you intend getting done. If you are in a strait, a very good indication as to choice—perhaps the best you could get—is a book you have a great curiosity about. You are then in the readiest and best of all possible conditions to improve by that book. It is analogous to what doctors tell us about the physical health and appetites of the patient. You must learn to distinguish between false appetite and real. There is such a thing as a false appetite, which will lead a man into vagaries with regard to diet, will tempt him to eat spicy things which he should not eat at all, and would not but that it is toothsome, and for the moment in baseness of mind. A man ought to inquire and find out what he really and truly has an appetite for—what suits his constitution ; and that, doctors tell him, is the very thing he ought to have in general. And so with books. As applicable to almost all of you, I will say that it is highly expedient to go into history—to inquire into what has passed before you in the families of men. The history

of the Romans and Greeks will first of all concern you ; and you will find that all the knowledge you have got will be extremely applicable
to elucidate that.    There you have the most
remarkable race of men in the world set before
you, to say nothing of the languages, which your
professors can better explain, and which, I believe, are admitted to be the most perfect orders
of speech we have yet found to exist among
men.    And you will find, if you read well, a
pair of extremely remarkable nations shining in
the records left by themselves as a kind of
pillar to light up life in the darkness of the past
ages ; and it will be well worth your while if
you can get into the understanding of what these
people were and what they did.    You will find a
great deal of hearsay, as I have found, that does
not touch on the matter ; but perhaps some of
you will get to see a Roman face to face ; you  .
will know in some measure how they contrived
to exist, and to perform these feats in the world ;

I believe, also, you will find a thing not much noted, that there was a very great deal of deep religion in its form in both nations. That is noted by the wisest of historians, and particularly by Ferguson, who is particularly well worth reading on Roman history; and I believe he was an alumnus in our own University. His book is a very creditable book. He points out the profoundly religious nature of the Roman people, notwithstanding the wildness and ferociousness of their nature. They believed that Jupiter Optimus—Jupiter Maximus—was lord of the universe, and that he had appointed the Romans to become the chief of men, provided they followed his commands—to brave all difficulty, and to stand up with an invincible front— to be ready to do and die ; and also to have the same sacred regard to veracity, to promise, to integrity, and all the virtues that surround that noblest quality of men—courage—to which the Romans gave the name of virtue, manhood, as the one thing ennobling for a man.

In the literary ages of Rome, that had very much decayed away; but still it had retained its place among the lower classes of the Roman people. Of the deeply religious nature of the Greeks, along with their beautiful and sunny effulgences of art, you have a striking proof, if you look for it.

In the tragedies of Sophocles, there is a most distinct recognition of the eternal justice of Heaven, and the unfailing punishment of crime against the laws of God.

I believe you will find in all histories that that has been at the head and foundation of them all, and that no nation that did not contemplate this wonderful universe with an awe-stricken and reverential feeling that there was a great unknown, omnipotent, and all-wise, and all-virtuous Being, superintending all men in it, and all interests in it—no nation ever came to very much, nor did any man either, who forgot that. If a man did forget that, he forgot the most important part of his mission in this world.

In our own history of England, which you will take a great deal of natural pains to make yourselves acquainted with, you will find it beyond all others worthy of your study ; because I believe that the British nation—and I include in them the Scottish nation—produced a finer set of men than any you will find it possible to get anywhere else in the world. (Applause.) I don't know in any history of Greece or Rome where you will get so fine a man as Oliver Cromwell. (Applause.) And we have had men worthy of memory in our little corner of the island here as well as others, and our history has been strong at least in being connected with the world itself—for if you examine well you will find that John Knox was the author, as it were, of Oliver Cromwell ; that the Puritan revolution would never have taken place in England at all if it had not been for that Scotchman. (Applause.) This is an arithmetical fact, and is not prompted by national vanity on my part at all.

(Laughter and applause.) And it is very possible, if you look at the struggle that was going on in England, as I have had to do in my time, you will see that people were overawed with the immense impediments lying in the way.

A small minority of God-fearing men in the country were flying away with any ship they could get to New England, rather than take the lion by the beard. They durstn't confront the powers with their most just complaint to be delivered from idolatry. They wanted to make the nation altogether conformable to the Hebrew Bible, which they understood to be according to the will of God ; and there could be no aim more legitimate. However, they could not have got their desire fulfilled at all if Knox had not succeeded by the firmness and nobleness of his mind. For he is also of the select of the earth to me—John Knox. (Applause.) What he has suffered from the ungrateful generations that have followed him should really make us humble

ourselves to the dust, to think that the most excellent man our country has produced, to whom
we owe everything that distinguishes us among
modern nations, should have been sneered at and
abused by people.   Knox was heard by Scotland
—the people heard him with the marrow of their
bones—they took up his doctrine, and they de-
fied principalities and powers to move them from
it.   "We must have it," they said.

It was at that time the Puritan struggle arose
in England, and you know well that the Scottish
Earls and nobility, with their tenantry, marched
away to Dunse-hill, and sat down there; and
just in the course of that struggle, when it was
either to be suppressed or brought into greater
vitality, they encamped on the top of Dunse-hill
thirty thousand armed men, drilled for that occasion, each regiment around its landlord, its earl,
or whatever he might be called, and eager for
Christ's Crown and Covenant.   That was the
signal for all England rising up into unappeas-

able determination to have the Gospel there
also, and you know it went on and came to be a
contest whether the Parliament or the King
should rule—whether it should be old formalities
and use and wont, or something that had been
of new conceived in the souls of men—namely,
a divine determination to walk according to the
laws of God here as the sum of all prosperity—
which of these should have the mastery ; and
after a long, long agony of struggle, it was
decided—the way we know.  I should say also
of that Protectorate of Oliver Cromwell's—notwithstanding the abuse it has encountered, and
the denial of everybody that it was able to get
on in the world, and so on—it appears to me to
have been the most salutary thing in the modern
history of England on the whole.  If Oliver
Cromwell had continued it out, I don't know
what it would have come to.  It would have got
corrupted perhaps in other hands, and could not
have gone on, but it was pure and true to the

last fibre in his mind—there was truth in it when he ruled over it.

Machiavelli has remarked, in speaking about the Romans, that democracy cannot exist anywhere in the world ; as a Government it is an impossibility that it should be continued, and he goes on proving that in his own way.  I do not ask you all to follow him in his conviction (hear) ; but it is to him a clear truth that it is a solecism and impossibility that the universal mass of men should govern themselves.  He says of the Romans that they continued a long time, but it was purely in virtue of this item in their constitution—namely, that they had all the conviction in their minds that it was solemnly necessary at times to appoint a Dictator—a man who had the power of life and death over everything—who degraded men out of their places, ordered them to execution, and did whatever seemed to him good in the name of God above him.  He was commanded to take care that the

Republic suffered no detriment, and Machiavelli calculates that that was the thing that purified the social system from time to time, and enabled it to hang on as it did—an extremely likely thing if it was composed of nothing but bad and tumultuous men triumphing in general over the better, and all going the bad road, in fact. Well, Oliver Cromwell's Protectorate, or Dictatorate if you will, lasted for about ten years, and you will find that nothing that was contrary to the laws of Heaven was allowed to live by Oliver. (A laugh, and applause.)   For example, it was found by his Parliament, called "Barebones"— the most zealous of all Parliaments probably— (laughter)—that the Court of Chancery in England was in a state that was really capable of no apology—no man could get up and say that that was a right court. There were, I think, fifteen thousand or fifteen hundred—(laughter) —I don't really remember which, but we shall call it by the last (renewed laughter)—there were fifteen hundred cases lying in it undecided; and one of them, I remember, for a large amount of money, was eighty-three years old, and it was going on still. Wigs were waving over it, and lawyers were taking their fees, and there was no end of it, upon which the Barebones people, after deliberation about it, thought it was expedient, and commanded by the Author of Man and the Fountain of Justice, and for the true and right, to abolish the court. Really, I don't know who could have dissented from that opinion. At the same time, it was thought by those who were wiser, and had more experience of the world, that it was a very dangerous thing, and would never suit at all. The lawyers began to make an immense noise about it. (Laughter.) All the public, the great mass of solid and well-disposed people who had got no deep insight into such matters, were very adverse to it, and the president of it, old Sir Francis Rous, who translated the Psalms—those that

we sing every Sunday in the church yet—a very
good man and a wise man—the Provost of Eton
—he got the minority, or I don't know whether
or no he did not persuade the majority—he, at
any rate, got a great number of the Parliament
to go to Oliver the Dictator, and lay down their
functions altogether, and declare officially with
their signature on Monday morning that the
Parliament was dissolved.

The thing was passed on Saturday night, and
on Monday morning Rous came and said,
"We cannot carry on the affair any longer, and
we remit it into the hands of your Highness."
Oliver in that way became Protector a second
time.

I give you this as an instance that Oliver felt
that the Parliament that had been dismissed had
been perfectly right with regard to Chancery,
and that there was no doubt of the propriety of
abolishing Chancery, or reforming it in some
kind of way. He considered it, and this is what

he did.  He assembled sixty of the wisest lawyers to be found in England.  Happily, there
were men great in the law—men who valued the
laws as much as anybody does now, I suppose.
(A laugh.)  Oliver said to them, " Go and examine this thing, and in the name of God inform
me what is necessary to be done with regard to
it.  You will see how we may clean out the foul
things in it that render it poison to everybody."
Well, they sat down then, and in the course of
six weeks—there was no public speaking then,
no reporting of speeches, and no trouble of any
kind ; there was just the business in hand—they
got sixty propositions fixed in their minds of
the things that required to be done.  And upon
these sixty propositions Chancery was reconsti-
tuted and remodelled, and so it has lasted to our
time.  It had become a nuisance, and could not
have continued much longer.

That is an instance of the manner in which
things were done when a Dictatorship prevailed

in the country, and that was what the Dictator did. Upon the whole, I do not think that, in general, out of common history books, you will ever get into the real history of this country, or anything particular which it would beseem you to know. You may read very ingenious and very clever books by men whom it would be the height of insolence in me to do any other thing than express my respect for. But their position is essentially sceptical. Man is unhappily in that condition that he will make only a temporary explanation of anything, and you will not be able, if you are like the man, to understand how this island came to be what it is. You will not find it recorded in books. You will find recorded in books a jumble of tumults, disastrous ineptitudes, and all that kind of thing. But to get what you want you will have to look into side sources, and inquire in all directions.

I remember getting Collins' *Peerage* to read—

a very poor peerage as a work of genius, but an
excellent book for diligence and fidelity—I was
writing on Oliver Cromwell at the time. (Applause.)   I could get no biographical dictionary,
and I thought the peerage book would help me,
at least tell me whether people were old or
young; and about all persons concerned in the
actions about which I wrote.   I got a great deal
of help out of poor Collins.   He was a diligent
and dark London bookseller of about a hundred
years ago, who compiled out of all kinds of
treasury chests, archives, books that were authentic, and out of all kinds of things out of
which he could get the information he wanted.
He was a very meritorious man.   I not only
found the solution of anything I wanted there,
but I began gradually to perceive this immense
fact, which I really advise every one of you who
read history to look out for and read for—if he
has not found it—it was that the kings of England all the way from the Norman Conquest

down to the times of Charles I. had appointed, so far as they knew, those who deserved to be appointed, peers. They were all Royal men, with minds full of justice and valour and humanity, and all kinds of qualities that are good for men to have who ought to rule over others. Then their genealogy was remarkable—and there is a great deal more in genealogies than is generally believed at present.

I never heard tell of any clever man that came out of entirely stupid people. If you look around the families of your acquaintance, you will see such cases in all directions. I know that it has been the case in mine. I can trace the father, and the son, and the grandson, and the family stamp is quite distinctly legible upon each of them, so that it goes for a great deal—the hereditary principle in Government as in other things; and it must be recognised so soon as there is any fixity in things.

You will remark that if at any time the genealogy of a peerage fails—if the man that actually holds the peerage is a fool in these earnest striking times, the man gets into mischief and gets into treason—he gets himself extinguished altogether, in fact. (Laughter.)

From these documents of old Collins it seems that a peer conducts himself in a solemn, good, pious, manly kind of way when he takes leave of life, and when he has hospitable habits, and is valiant in his procedure throughout; and that in general a King, with a noble approximation to what was right, had nominated this man, saying "Come you to me, sir; come out of the common level of the people, where you are liable to be trampled upon; come here and take a district of country and make it into your own image more or less; be a king under me, and understand that that is your function." I say this is the most divine thing that a human being can do to other human beings, and no kind of being whatever has so much of the character of

God Almighty's Divine Government as that thing we see that went all over England, and that is the grand soul of England's history.

It is historically true that down to the time of Charles I., it was not understood that any man was made a peer without having a merit in him to constitute him a proper subject for a peerage. In Charles I.'s time it grew to be known or said that if a man was by birth a gentleman, and was worth £10,000 a-year, and bestowed his gifts up and down among courtiers, he could be made a peer. Under Charles II. it went on with still more rapidity, and has been going on with ever increasing velocity until we see the perfect break-neck pace at which they are now going. (A laugh.) And now a peerage is a paltry kind of thing to what it was in these old times. I could go into a great many more details about things of that sort, but I must turn to another branch of the subject.

One remark more about your reading. I do

not know whether it has been sufficiently brought home to you that there are two kinds of books. When a man is reading on any kind of subject, in most departments of books—in all books, if you take it in a wide sense—you will find that there is a division of good books and bad books—there is a good kind of a book and a bad kind of a book. I am not to assume that you are all ill acquainted with this; but I may remind you that it is a very important consideration at present. It casts aside altogether the idea that people have that if they are reading any book—that if an ignorant man is reading any book, he is doing rather better than nothing at all. I entirely call that in question. I even venture to deny it. (Laughter and cheers.) It would be much safer and better would he have no concern with books at all than with some of them. You know these are my views. There are a number, an increasing number, of books that are decidedly to him not useful. (Hear.) But he will learn also that a certain number of books were written by a supreme, noble kind of people—not a very great number—but a great number adhere more or less to that side of things. In short, as I have written it down somewhere else, I conceive that books are like men's souls—divided into sheep and goats. (Laughter and applause.) Some of them are calculated to be of very great advantage in teaching—in forwarding the teaching of all generations. Others are going down, down, doing more and more, wilder and wilder mischief.

And for the rest, in regard to all your studies here, and whatever you may learn, you are to remember that the object is not particular knowledge—that you are going to get higher in technical perfections, and all that sort of thing. There is a higher aim lies at the rear of all that, especially among those who are intended for literary, for speaking pursuits—the sacred profession. You are ever to bear in mind

that there lies behind that the acquisition of
what may be called wisdom—namely, sound
appreciation and just decision as to all the objects that come round about you, and the habit of
behaving with justice and wisdom. In short, great
is wisdom—great is the value of wisdom. It cannot be exaggerated. The highest achievement of
man—"Blessed is he that getteth understanding." And that, I believe, occasionally may be
missed very easily ; but never more easily than
now, I think. If that is a failure, all is a
failure. However, I will not touch further upon
that matter.

In this University I learn from many sides
that there is a great and considerable stir about
endowments. Oh, I should have said in regard
to book reading, if it be so very important, how
very useful would an excellent library be in
every University. I hope that will not be neglected by those gentlemen who have charge of
you—and, indeed, I am happy to hear that your

library is very much improved since the time I
knew it ; and I hope it will go on improving
more and more. You require money to do that,
and you require also judgment in the selectors
of the books—pious insight into what is really
for the advantage of human souls, and the ex-
clusion of all kinds of clap-trap books which
merely excite the astonishment of foolish people. (Laughter.) Wise books—as much as possible good books.

As I was saying, there appears to be a great
demand for endowments — an assiduous and
praiseworthy industry for getting new funds
collected for encouraging the ingenious youth
of Universities, especially in this the chief University of the country. (Hear, hear.) Well, I
entirely participate in everybody's approval of
the movement. It is very desirable. It should
be responded to, and one expects most assuredly
will. At least, if it is not, it will be shameful to
the country of Scotland, which never was so rich

in money as at the present moment, and never
stood so much in need of getting noble Universities to counteract many influences that are
springing up alongside of money. It should not
be backward in coming forward in the way of
endowments (a laugh)—at least, in rivalry to our
rude old barbarous ancestors, as we have been
pleased to call them. Such munificence as
theirs is beyond all praise, to whom I am sorry
to say we are not yet by any manner of means
equal or approaching equality. (Laughter.)
There is an overabundance of money, and sometimes I cannot help thinking that, probably,
never has there been at any other time in Scotland the hundredth part of the money that now
is, or even the thousandth part, for wherever I
go there is that gold-nuggeting (a laugh)—that
prosperity.

Many men are counting their balances by
millions. Money was never so abundant, and
nothing that is good to be done with it. ("Hear,

hear," and a laugh.) No man knows—or very few men know—what benefit to get out of his money. In fact, it too often is secretly a curse to him. Much better for him never to have had any. But I do not expect that generally to be believed. (Laughter.) Nevertheless, I should think it a beautiful relief to any man that has an honest purpose struggling in him to bequeath a handsome house of refuge, so to speak, for some meritorious man who may hereafter be born into the world, to enable him a little to get on his way. To do, in fact, as those old Norman kings whom I have described to you—to raise a man out of the dirt and mud where he is getting trampled, unworthily on his part, into some kind of position where he may acquire the power to do some good in his generation. I hope that as much as possible will be done in that way; that efforts will not be relaxed till the thing is in a satisfactory state. At the same time, in regard to the classical department of things, it is to be desired that it were properly supported—that we could allow people to go and devote more leisure possibly to the cultivation of particular departments.

We might have more of this from Scotch Universities than we have. I am bound, however, to say that it does not appear as if of late times endowment was the real soul of the matter. The English, for example, are the richest people for endowments on the face of the earth in their Universities; and it is a remarkable fact that since the time of Bentley you cannot name anybody that has gained a great name in scholarship among them, or constituted a point of revolution in the pursuits of men in that way. The man that did that is a man worthy of being remembered among men, although he may be a poor man, and not endowed with worldly wealth. One man that actually did constitute a revolution was the son of a poor weaver in Saxony, who edited his " Tibullus" in Dresden in the room of a poor comrade, and who, while he was editing his "Tibullus," had to gather his pease-cod shells on the streets and boil them for his dinner. That was his endowment. But he was recognised soon to have done a great thing. His name was Heyne.

I can remember it was quite a revolution in my mind when I got hold of that man's book on Virgil. I found that for the first time I had understood him—that he had introduced me for the first time into an insight of Roman life, and pointed out the circumstances in which these were written, and here was interpretation; and it has gone on in all manner of development, and has spread out into other countries.

Upon the whole, there is one reason why endowments are not given now as they were in old days, when they founded abbeys, colleges, and all kinds of things of that description, with such success as we know. All that has changed

now. Why that has decayed away may in part
be that people have become doubtful that colleges are now the real sources of that which I
call wisdom, whether they are anything more—
anything much more—than a cultivating of man
in the specific arts. In fact, there has been a
suspicion of that kind in the world for a long
time. (A laugh.) That is an old saying, an
old proverb, "An ounce of mother wit is worth
a pound of clergy." (Laughter.) There is a
suspicion that a man is perhaps not nearly so
wise as he looks, or because he has poured out
speech so copiously. (Laughter.)

When the seven free Arts on which the old
Universities were based came to be modified a
little, in order to be convenient for or to pro-
mote the wants of modern society—though,
perhaps, some of them are obsolete enough even
yet for some of us—there arose a feeling that
mere vocality, mere culture of speech, if that is
what comes out of a man, though he may be a

great speaker, an eloquent orator, yet there is
no real substance there—if that is what was required and aimed at by the man himself, and by
the community that set him upon becoming a
learned man.    Maid-servants, I hear people
complaining, are getting instructed in the "olo-
gies," and so on, and are apparently totally ignorant of brewing, boiling, and baking (laughter) ;
above all things, not taught what is necessary
to be known, from the highest to the lowest—
strict obedience, humility, and correct moral
conduct.    Oh, it is a dismal chapter, all that, if
one went into it !

What has been done by rushing after fine
speech ?  I have written down some very fierce
things about that, perhaps considerably more
emphatic than I would wish them to be now ;
but they are deeply my conviction.    (Hear,
hear.)  There is very great necessity indeed of
getting a little more silent than we are.    It
seems to me the finest nations of the world—

the English and the American—are going all
away into wind and tongue. (Applause and
laughter.) But it will appear sufficiently tragical
by-and-bye, long after I am away out of it.
Silence is the eternal duty of a man. He wont
get to any real understanding of what is com-
plex, and, what is more than any other, perti-
nent to his interests, without maintaining silence.
"Watch the tongue," is a very old precept, and
a most true one. I do not want to discourage
any of you from your Demosthenes, and your
studies of the niceties of language, and all that.
Believe me, I value that as much as any of you.
I consider it a very graceful thing, and a proper
thing, for every human creature to know what
the implement which he uses in communicating
his thoughts is, and how to make the very utmost of it. I want you to study Demosthenes,
and know all his excellencies. At the same
time, I must say that speech does not seem to
me, on the whole, to have turned to any good
account.

Why tell me that a man is a fine speaker if it is not the truth that he is speaking ? Phocion, who did not speak at all, was a great deal nearer hitting the mark than Demosthenes. (Laughter.) He used to tell the Athenians—"You can't fight Philip. You have not the slightest chance with him. He is a man who holds his tongue ; he has great disciplined armies ; he can brag anybody you like in your cities here ; and he is going on steadily with an unvarying aim towards his object : and he will infallibly beat any kind of men such as you, going on raging from shore to shore with all that rampant nonsense." Demosthenes said to him one day—"The Athenians will get mad some day and kill you." "Yes," Phocion says, "when they are mad ; and you as soon as they get sane again." (Laughter.)

It is also told about him going to Messina on some deputation that the Athenians wanted on some kind of matter of an intricate and contentious nature, that Phocion went with some story in his mouth to speak about. He was a man of few words—no unveracity ; and after he had gone on telling the story a certain time there was one burst of interruption. One man interrupted with something he tried to answer, and then another ; and, finally, the people began bragging and bawling, and no end of debate, till it ended in the want of power in the people to say any more. Phocion drew back altogether, struck dumb, and would not speak another word to any man ; and he left it to them to decide in any way they liked.

It appears to me there is a kind of eloquence in that which is equal to anything Demosthenes ever said—" Take your own way, and let me out altogether." (Applause.)

All these considerations, and manifold more connected with them—innumerable considerations, resulting from observation of the world at this moment—have led many people to doubt of the salutary effect of vocal education altogether. I do not mean to say it should be entirely excluded; but I look to something that will take hold of the matter much more closely, and not allow it slip out of our fingers, and remain worse than it was. For if a good speaker—an eloquent speaker—is not speaking the truth, is there a more horrid kind of object in creation? (Loud cheers.) Of such speech I hear all manner and kind of people say it is excellent; but I care very little about how he said it, provided I understand it, and it be true. Excellent speaker! but what if he is telling me things that are untrue, that are not the fact about it—if he has formed a wrong judgment about it—if he has no judgment in his mind to form a right conclusion in regard to the matter? An excellent speaker of that kind is, as it were, saying—" Ho, every one that wants to be persuaded of the thing that is not true, come hither." (Great laughter and applause.) I would recommend you to be very chary of that kind of excellent speech.   (Renewed laughter.)

Well, all that being the too well-known product of our method of vocal education—the mouth merely operating on the tongue of the pupil, and teaching him to wag it in a particular way (laughter)—it had made a great many thinking men entertain a very great distrust of this not very salutary way of procedure, and they have longed for some kind of practical way of working out the business.   There would be room for a great deal of description about it if I went into it; but I must content myself with saying that the most remarkable piece of reading that you may be recommended to take and try if you can study is a book by Goethe—one of his last books, which he wrote when he was an old man, about seventy years of age—I think one of the most beautiful he ever wrote, full of mild wisdom, and which is found to be very touching by those who have eyes to discern and

hearts to feel it. It is one of the·pieces in
"Wilhelm Meister's Travels." I read it through
many years ago ; and, of course, I had to read
into it very hard when I was translating it
(applause), and it has always dwelt in my mind
as about the most remarkable bit of writing that
I have known to be executed in these late centuries. I have often said, there are ten pages
of that which, if ambition had been my only
rule, I would rather have written than have
written all the books that have appeared since I
came into the world. (Cheers.) Deep, deep is
the meaning of what is said there. They turn
on the Christian religion and the religious phenomena of Christian life—altogether sketched
out in the most airy, graceful, delicately-wise
kind of way, so as to keep himself out of the
common controversies of the street and of the
forum, yet to indicate what was the result of
things he had been long meditating upon.
Among others, he introduces, in an aërial, flighty

kind of way, here and there a touch which grows into a beautiful picture—a scheme of entirely mute education, at least with no more speech than is absolutely necessary for what they have to do.

Three of the wisest men that can be got are met to consider what is the function which transcends all others in importance to build up the young generation, which shall be free from all that perilous stuff that has been weighing us down and clogging every step, and which is the only thing we can hope to go on with if we would leave the world a little better, and not the worse of our having been in it for those who are to follow. The man who is the eldest of the three says to Goethe, "You give by nature to the well-formed children you bring into the world a great many precious gifts, and very frequently these are best of all developed by nature herself, with a very slight assistance where assistance is seen to be wise and profitable, and forbearance very

often on the part of the overlooker of the process of education ; but there is one thing that no
child brings into the world with it, and without
which all other things are of no use."   Wilhelm,
who is there beside him, says, "What is that?"
"All who enter the world want it," says the
eldest ; "perhaps you yourself."   Wilhelm says,
"Well, tell me what it is."   "It is," says the
eldest,   " reverence — *Ehrfurcht* — Reverence !
Honour done to those who are grander and
better than you, without fear; distinct from
fear."   *Ehrfurcht*—"the soul of all religion that
ever has been among men, or ever will be."   And
he goes into practicality.   He practically distinguishes the kinds of religion that are in the
world, and he makes out three reverences.   The
boys are all trained to go through certain gesti-
culations, to lay their hands on their breast and
look up to heaven, and they give their three
reverences.   The first and simplest is that of
reverence for what is above us.   It is the soul of

all the Pagan religions ; there is nothing better in man than that. Then there is reverence for what is around us or about us—reverence for our equals, and to which he attributes an immense power in the culture of man. The third is reverence for what is beneath us—to learn to recognise in pain, sorrow, and contradiction, even in those things, odious as they are to flesh and blood—to learn that there lies in these a priceless blessing. And he defines that as being the soul of the Christian religion—the highest of all religions ; a height, as Goethe says—and that is very true, even to the letter, as I consider—a height to which the human species was fated and enabled to attain, and from which, having once attained it, it can never retrograde. It cannot descend down below that permanently, Goethe's idea is.

Often one thinks it was good to have a faith of that kind—that always, even in the most degraded, sunken, and unbelieving times, he calculates there will be found some few souls who will recognise what that meant ; and that the world, having once received it, there is no fear of its retrograding. He goes on then to tell us the way in which they seek to teach boys, in the sciences particularly, whatever the boy is fit for. Wilhelm left his own boy there, expecting they would make him a Master of Arts, or something of that kind ; and when he came back for him he saw a thundering cloud of dust coming over the plain, of which he could make nothing. It turned out to be a tempest of wild horses, managed by young lads who had a turn for hunting with their grooms. His own son was among them, and he found that the breaking of colts was the thing he was most suited for. (Laughter.) This is what Goethe calls Art, which I should not make clear to you by any definition unless it is clear already. (A laugh.) I would not attempt to define it as music, painting, and poetry, and so on ; it is in quite a higher sense than the common one, and in which, I am afraid, most of our painters, poets, and music men would not pass muster. (A laugh.) He considers that the highest pitch to which human culture can go ; and he watches with great industry how it is to be brought about with men who have a turn for it.

Very wise and beautiful it is. It gives one an idea that something greatly better is possible for man in the world. I confess it seems to me it is a shadow of what will come, unless the world is to come to a conclusion that is perfectly frightful ; some kind of scheme of education like that, presided over by the wisest and most sacred men that can be got in the world, and watching from a distance—a training in practicality at every turn ; no speech in it except that speech that is to be followed by action, for that ought to be the rule as nearly as possible among them. For rarely should men speak at all unless it is to say that thing that is to be done ; and let him

go and do his part in it, and to say no more
about it.  I should say there is nothing in the
world you can conceive so difficult, *prima facie*,
as that of getting a set of men gathered together — rough, rude, and ignorant people —
gather them together, promise them a shilling a
day, rank them up, give them very severe and
sharp drill, and by bullying and drill—for the
word "drill" seems as if it meant the treatment
that would force them to learn—they learn what
it is necessary to learn ; and there is the man, a
piece of an animated machine, a wonder of
wonders to look at.  He will go and obey one
man, and walk into the cannon's mouth for him,
and do anything whatever that is commanded of
him by his general officer.  And I believe all
manner of things in this way could be done if
there were anything like the same attention
bestowed.  Very many things could be regi-
mented and organized into the mute system of
education that Goethe evidently adumbrates

there. But I believe, when people look into it, it will be found that they will not be very long in trying to make some efforts in that direction ; for the saving of human labour, and the avoidance of human misery, would be uncountable if it were set about and begun even in part.

Alas ! it is painful to think how very far away it is—any fulfilment of such things ; for I need not hide from you, young gentlemen—and that is one of the last things I am going to tell you —that you have got into a very troublous epoch of the world ; and I don't think you will find it improve the footing you have, though you have many advantages which we had not. You have careers open to you, by public examinations and so on, which is a thing much to be approved, and which we hope to see perfected more and more. All that was entirely unknown in my time, and you have many things to recognise as advantages. But you will find the ways of the world more anarchical than ever, I think. As far as I have noticed, revolution has come upon us. We have got into the age of revolutions. All kinds of things are coming to be subjected to fire, as it were; hotter and hotter the wind rises around everything.

Curious to say, now in Oxford and other places that used to seem to lie at anchor in the stream of time, regardless of all changes, they are getting into the highest humour of mutation, and all sorts of new ideas are getting afloat. It is evident that whatever is not made of asbestos will have to be burnt in this world. It will not stand the heat it is getting exposed to. And in saying that, it is but saying in other words that we are in an epoch of anarchy—anarchy *plus* the constable. (Laughter.) There is nobody that picks one's pocket without some policeman being ready to take him up. (Renewed laughter.) But in every other thing he is the son, not of Kosmos, but of Chaos. He is a disobedient, and

11

reckless, and altogether a waste kind of object— a commonplace man in these epochs ; and the wiser kind of man—the select, of whom I hope you will be part—has more and more a set time to it to look forward, and will require to move with double wisdom ; and will find, in short, that the crooked things that he has to pull straight in his own life, or round about, wherever he may be, are manifold, and will task all his strength wherever he may go.

But why should I complain of that either ?— for that is a thing a man is born to in all epochs. He is born to expend every particle of strength that God Almighty has given him, in doing the work he finds he is fit for—to stand it out to the last breath of life, and do his best. We are called upon to do that ; and the reward we all get—which we are perfectly sure of if we have merited it—is that we have got the work done, or, at least, that we have tried to do the work ; for that is a great blessing in itself; and

I should say there is not very much more
reward than that going in this world. If the
man gets meat and clothes, what matters it
whether he have £10,000, or £10,000,000, or £70
a-year. He can get meat and clothes for that;
and he will find very little difference intrinsically, if he is a wise man.

I warmly second the advice of the wisest of
men—"Don't be ambitious; don't be at all
too desirous to success; be loyal and modest."
Cut down the proud towering thoughts that you
get into you, or see they be pure as well as high.
There is a nobler ambition than the gaining of
all California would be, or the getting of all the
suffrages that are on the planet just now. (Loud
and prolonged cheers.)

Finally, gentlemen, I have one advice to give
you, which is practically of very great importance, though a very humble one.

I have no doubt you will have among you
people ardently bent to consider life cheap, for

the purpose of getting forward in what they are aiming at of high; and you are to consider throughout, much more than is done at present, that health is a thing to be attended to continually—that you are to regard that as the very highest of all temporal things for you. (Applause.) There is no kind of achievement you could make in the world that is equal to perfect health. What are nuggets and millions? The French financier said, "Alas! why is there no sleep to be sold?" Sleep was not in the market at any quotation. (Laughter and applause.)

It is a curious thing that I remarked long ago, and have often turned in my head, that the old word for "holy" in the German language—*heilig*—also means "healthy." And so *Heilbronn* means "holy-well," or "healthy-well." We have in the Scotch "hale;" and, I suppose our English word "whole"—with a "w"—all of one piece, without any hole in it—is the same word. I find that you could not get any better definition of what "holy" really is than "healthy—completely healthy." *Mens sana in corpore sano.* (Applause.)

A man with his intellect a clear, plain, geometric mirror, brilliantly sensitive of all objects and impressions around it, and imagining all things in their correct proportions—not twisted up into convex or concave, and distorting everything, so that he cannot see the truth of the matter without endless groping and manipulation—healthy, clear, and free, and all round about him. We never can attain that at all. In fact, the operations we have got into are destructive of it. You cannot, if you are going to do any decisive intellectual operation—if you are going to write a book—at least, I never could—without getting decidedly made ill by it, and really you must if it is your business—and you must follow out what you are at—and it sometimes is at the expense of health. Only remember at all times to get back as fast as

possible out of it into health, and regard the real
equilibrium as the centre of things. You should
always look at the *heilig*, which means holy, and
holy means healthy.

Well, that old etymology—what a lesson it
is against certain gloomy, austere, ascetic
people, that have gone about as if this world
were all a dismal-prison house! It has, indeed,
got all the ugly things in it that I have been
alluding to ; but there is an eternal sky over it,
and the blessed sunshine, verdure of spring, and
rich autumn, and all that in it, too. Piety does
not mean that a man should make a sour face
about things, and refuse to enjoy in moderation
what his Maker has given. Neither do you
find it to have been so with old Knox. If you
look into him you will find a beautiful Scotch
humour in him, as well as the grimmest and
sternest truth when necessary, and a great deal
of laughter. We find really some of the sun-
niest glimpses of things come out of Knox that

I have seen in any man; for instance, in his
" History of the Reformation," which is a book
I hope every one of you will read—a glorious
book.

On the whole, I would bid you stand up to
your work, whatever it may be, and not be
afraid of it—not in sorrows or contradiction to
yield, but pushing on towards the goal.  And
don't suppose that people are hostile to you in
the world.  You will rarely find anybody de-
signedly doing you ill.  You may feel often as
if the whole world is obstructing you, more or
less; but you will find that to be because the
world is travelling in a different way from you,
and rushing on in its own path.  Each man has
only an extremely good-will to himself—which
he has a right to have—and is moving on towards his object.  Keep out of literature as a
general rule, I should say also.  (Laughter.)
If you find many people who are hard and indifferent to you in a world that you consider

to be unhospitable and cruel—as often, indeed, happens to a tender-hearted, stirring young creature—you will also find there are noble hearts who will look kindly on you, and their help will be precious to you beyond price. You will get good and evil as you go on, and have the success that has been appointed to you.

I will wind up with a small bit of verse that is from Goethe also, and has often gone through my mind. To me it has the tone of a modern psalm in it in some measure. It is sweet and clear. The clearest of sceptical men had not anything like so clear a mind as that man had —freer from cant and misdirected notion of any kind than any man in these ages has been. This is what the poet says :—

> The Future hides in it
> Gladness and sorrow :
> We press still thorow ;
> Nought that abides in it
> Daunting us—Onward !

And solemn before us,
Veiled, the dark Portal,
Goal of all mortal.
Stars silent rest o'er us—
Graves under us, silent.

While earnest thou gazest
Comes boding of terror,
Come phantasm and error;
Perplexes the bravest
With doubt and misgiving.

But heard are the voices,
Heard are the Sages,
The Worlds and the Ages:
"Choose well: your choice is
Brief, and yet endless."

Here eyes do regard you
In Eternity's stillness;
Here is all fulness,
Ye brave, to reward you.
Work, and despair not.*

---

* Originally published in Carlyle's "Past and Present,"
(Lond. 1843,) p. 318, and introduced there by the following
words :—

"My candid readers, we will march out of this Third Book
with a rhythmic word of Goethe's on our tongue; a word which

One last word.  *Wir heissen euch hoffen*—we
bid you be of hope.   Adieu for this time.

---

perhaps has already sung itself, in dark hours and in bright,
through many a heart.  To me, finding it devout yet wholly
credible and veritable, full of piety yet free of cant; to me
joyfully finding much in it, and joyfully missing so much in it,
this little snatch of music, by the greatest German man, sounds
like a stanza in the grand *Road Song* and *Marching Song* of our
great Teutonic kindred,—wending, wending, valiant and victorious, through the undiscovered Deeps of Time !"

The original runs as follows :—

> Die Zukunft decket
> Schmerzen und Glücke.
> Schrittweis' dem Blicke,
> Doch ungeschrecket
> Dringen wir vorwärts.

> Und schwer und schwerer
> Hängt eine Hülle
> Mit Ehrfurcht.   Stille
> Ruhn oben die Sterne
> Und unten die Gräber.

> Betracht' sie genauer
> Und siehe, so melden
> Im Busen der Helden
> Sich wandelnde Schauer
> Und ernste Gefühle.

Doch rufen von drüben
Die Stimmen der Geister
Die Stimmen der Meister :
Versäumt nicht zu üben
Die Kräfte des Guten.

Hier winden sich Kronen
In ewiger Stille,
Die sollen mit Fülle
Die Thätigen lohnen !
Wir heissen euch hoffen.

# THE MORAL PHILOSOPHY CHAIR IN
# EDINBURGH UNIVERSITY.

—o—

THE following is a letter addressed by Mr. Carlyle to Dr. Hutchison Stirling, late one of the candidates for the Chair of Moral Philosophy in the University of Edinburgh :—

"Chelsea, 16th June, 1868.

"DEAR STIRLING,—

"YOU well know how reluctant I have been to interfere at all in the election now close on us, and that in stating, as bound, what my own clear knowledge of your qualities was, I have strictly held by that, and abstained from more. But the news I now have from Edin-

burgh is of such a complexion, so dubious, and
so surprising to me ; and I now find I shall pri-
vately have so much regret in a certain event—
which seems to be reckoned possible, and to
depend on one gentleman of the seven—that, to
secure my own conscience in the matter, a few
plainer words seem needful.    To whatever I
have said of you already, therefore, I now volun-
teer to add, that I think you not only the one
man in Britain capable of bringing Metaphysical
Philosophy, in the ultimate, German or European, and highest actual form of it, distinctly
home to the understanding of British men who
wish to understand it, but that I notice in you
farther, on the moral side, a sound strength of
intellectual discernment, a noble valour and
reverence of mind, which seems to me to mark
you out as the man capable of doing us the
highest service in Ethical science too : that of
restoring, or decisively beginning to restore, the
doctrine of morals to what I must ever reckon

its one true and everlasting basis (namely, the divine or supra-sensual one), and thus of victoriously reconciling and rendering identical the latest dictates of modern science with the earliest dawnings of wisdom among the race of men.

"This is truly my opinion, and how important to me, not for the sake of Edinburgh University alone, but of the whole world for ages to come, I need not say to you! I have not the honour of any personal acquaintance with Mr. Adam Black, late member for Edinburgh, but for fifty years back have known him, in the distance, and by current and credible report, as a man of solid sense, independence, probity, and public spirit; and if, in your better knowledge of the circumstances, you judge it suitable to read this note to him—to him, or indeed to any other person—you are perfectly at liberty to do so.

"Yours sincerely always,

"T. CARLYLE."

# FAREWELL LETTER TO THE STUDENTS.

MR. CARLYLE, ex-Lord Rector of the University of Edinburgh, being asked before the expiration of his term of office, to deliver a valedictory address to the students, he sent the following letter to Mr. Robertson, Vice-President of the Committee for his election :—

"Chelsea, December 6, 1868.

" DEAR SIR,—

" I MUCH regret that a valedictory speech from me, in present circumstances, is a thing I must not think of. Be pleased to advise the young gentlemen who were so friendly towards me that I have already sent them, in silence, but with emotions deep enough, perhaps too deep, my loving farewell, and that ingratitude or want of regard is by no means among the causes that keep me absent. With a fine youthful enthusiasm, beautiful to look upon, they bestowed on me that bit of honour, loyally all they had ; and it has now, for reasons one and another, become touchingly memorable to me—touchingly, and even grandly and tragically—never to be forgotten for the remainder of my life. Bid them, in my name, if they still love me, fight the good fight, and quit themselves like men in the warfare to which they are as if conscript and consecrated, and which lies ahead. Tell them to consult the eternal oracles (not yet inaudible, nor ever to become so, when worthily inquired of) ; and to disregard, nearly altogether, in comparison, the temporary noises, menacings, and deliriums. May they love wisdom, as wisdom, if she is to yield her treasures, must be loved, piously, valiantly, humbly, beyond life itself, or the prizes of life, with all one's heart and all one's soul. In that case (I will say again), and not in any other case, it shall be well with them.

"Adieu, my young friends, a long adieu, yours with great sincerity,

"T. CARLYLE."

# INDEX.

THE END

BILLING AND SONS, PRINTERS, GUILDFORD, SURREY.

*July*, 1878.

# CHATTO & WINDUS'S

## List of Books.

# ON BOOKS AND BOOK-BUYERS.

## By John Ruskin, LL.D.

" *I say we have despised literature ; what do we, as a nation, care about books ? How much do you think we spend altogether on our libraries, public or private, as compared with what we spend on our horses ? If a man spends lavishly on his library, you call him mad —a bibliomaniac. But you never call one a horse-maniac, though men ruin themselves every day by their horses, and you do not hear of people ruining themselves by their books. Or, to go lower still, how much do you think the contents of the book-shelves of the United Kingdom, public and private, would fetch, as compared with the contents of its wine-cellars ? What position would its expenditure on literature take as com-pared with its expenditure on luxurious eating ? We talk of food for the mind, as of food for the body : now, a good book contains such food inexhaustible : it is provision for life, and for the best part of us ; yet how long most people would look at the best book before they would give the price of a large turbot for it ! Though there have been men who have pinched their stomachs and bared their backs to buy a book, whose libraries were cheaper to them, I think, in the end, than most men's dinners are. We are few of us put to such a trial, and more the pity ; for, indeed, a precious thing is all the more precious to us if it has been won by work or economy ; and if public libraries were half as costly as public dinners, or books cost the tenth part of what bracelets do, even foolish men and women might sometimes suspect there was good in read-ing as well as in munching and sparkling ; whereas the very cheapness of literature is making even wiser people forget that if a book is worth reading it is worth buying.*"—Sesame and Lilies ; or, King's Treasures.*

# Chatto & Windus's

## List of Books.

Square 8vo, cloth, extra gilt, gilt edges, with Coloured Frontispiece and numerous Illustrations, 10s. 6d.

### The Art of Beauty.

By Mrs. H. R. HAWEIS, Author of "Chaucer for Children." With nearly One Hundred Illustrations by the Author.

"*A most interesting book, full of valuable hints and suggestions. . . . . If young ladies would but lend their ears for a little to Mrs. Haweis, we are quite sure that it would result in their being at once more tasteful, more happy, and more healthy than they now often are, with their false hair, high heels, tight corsets, and ever so much else of the same sort.*"—NONCONFORMIST.

Crown 4to, containing 24 Plates beautifully printed in Colours, with descriptive Text, cloth extra, gilt, 6s. ; illustrated boards, 3s. 6d.

### Æsop's Fables

Translated into Human Nature. By C. H. BENNETT.

"*For fun and frolic the new version of Æsop's Fables must bear away the palm. There are plenty of grown-up children who like to be amused ; and if this new version of old stories does not amuse them they must be very dull indeed, and their situation one much to be commiserated.*"—MORNING POST.

Crown 8vo, cloth extra, with 639 Illustrations, 7s. 6d., a New Edition (uniform with "The Englishman's House") of

### A Handbook of Architectural Styles.

Translated from the German of A. ROSENGARTEN by W. COLLETT-SANDARS. With 639 Illustrations.

Crown 8vo, Coloured Frontispiece and Illustrations, cloth gilt, 7s. 6d.

# A History of Advertising,

From the Earliest Times. Illustrated by Anecdotes, Curious Specimens, and Biographical Notes of Successful Advertisers. By HENRY SAMPSON.

" We have here a book to be thankful for. We recommend the present volume, which takes us through antiquity, the middle ages, and the present time, illustrating all in turn by advertisements—serious, comic, roguish, or downright rascally. The volume is full of entertainment from the first page to the last."—ATHENÆUM.

Crown 8vo, with Portrait and Facsimile, cloth extra, 7s. 6d.

# Artemus Ward's Works:

The Works of CHARLES FARRER BROWNE, better known as ARTEMUS WARD. With Portrait, facsimile of Handwriting, &c.

" The author combines the powers of Thackeray with those of Albert Smith. The salt is rubbed in with a native hand—one which has the gift of tickling."— SATURDAY REVIEW.

Small 4to, green and gold, 6s. 6d.; gilt edges, 7s. 6d.

# As Pretty as Seven,

and other Popular German Stories. Collected by LUDWIG BECHSTEIN. With Additional Tales by the Brothers GRIMM, and 100 Illustrations by RICHTER.

Crown 8vo, cloth extra, 7s. 6d.

# A Handbook of London Bankers;

With some Account of their Predecessors, the Early Goldsmiths; together with Lists of Bankers, from 1677 to 1876. By F. G. HILTON PRICE.

Crown 8vo, cloth extra, 9s.

# Bardsley's Our English Surnames:

Their Sources and Significations. By CHARLES WAREING BARDSLEY, M.A. Second Edition, revised throughout, considerably enlarged, and partially rewritten.

" Mr. Bardsley has faithfully consulted the original mediæval documents and works from which the origin and development of surnames can alone be satisfactorily traced. He has furnished a valuable contribution to the literature of surnames, and we hope to hear more of him in this field."—TIMES.

Demy 8vo, cloth extra, with Illustrations, 18s.

# Baker's Clouds in the East:

Travels and Adventures on the Perso-Turkoman Frontier. By VALENTINE BAKER. With Maps and Illustrations, coloured and plain, from Original Sketches. Second Edition, revised and corrected.

" A man who not only thinks for himself, but who has risked his life in order to gain information. . . . A most graphic and lively narrative of travels and adventures which have nothing of the commonplace about them."—LEEDS MERCURY.

Demy 8vo, illustrated, uniform in size for binding.

# *Henry Blackburn's Art Handbooks:*

### *Academy Notes,* 1875.
With Forty Illustrations. 1*s.*

### *Academy Notes,* 1876.
With One Hundred and Seven Illustrations. 1*s.*

### *Academy Notes,* 1877.
With One Hundred and Forty-three Illustrations. 1*s.*

### *Academy Notes,* 1878.
With One Hundred and Fifty Illustrations. 1*s.*

### *Grosvenor Notes,* 1878.
With Sixty-eight Illustrations. 1*s.* [*See end of this list.*

### *Dudley Notes,* 1878.
(The Water-colour Exhibition.) With Sixty-four Illusts., 1*s.*

### *Pictures at South Kensington.*
(The Raphael Cartoons, Sheepshanks Collection, &c.) With Seventy Illustrations. 1*s.*

### *The English Pictures at the National Gallery.*
With One Hundred and Fourteen Illustrations. 1*s.*

### *The Old Masters at the National Gallery.*
With One Hundred and Thirty Illustrations. 1*s.* 6*d.*

*\*\** The two last form a complete Catalogue to the National Gallery, and may be had bound in one volume, cloth, 3*s.*

*Other parts in preparation.*

"*Our Bank of Elegance notes are not in high credit. But our Bank of Arts notes ought to be, when the bank is* HENRY BLACKBURN'S & Co., *and the notes are his Grosvenor Gallery Notes, and his Academy Notes for* 1878. *Never were more unmistakable cases of "value received," than theirs who purchase these two wonderful shillingsworths—the best aids to memory, for the collections they relate to, that have ever been produced. The Illustrations, excellent records of the pictures, in many cases from sketches by the painters, are full of spirit, and, for their scale, wonderfully effective; the remarks terse, and to the point. After Punch's Own Guide to the Academy, and the Grosvenor, the best, he has no hesitation in saying, are Mr. Blackburn's.*"—PUNCH, *June 7,* 1878.

*UNIFORM WITH "ACADEMY NOTES."*

### *The Royal Scottish Academy Notes,* 1878.
Containing One Hundred and Seventeen Illustrations of the Chief Works, from Drawings by the Artists. Edited by GEORGE R. HALKETT. 1*s.*

### *Notes to the Seventeenth Exhibition of the Glasgow*
*Institute of the Fine Arts,* 1878. Containing 95 Illustrations, chiefly from Drawings by the Artists. Edited by GEORGE R. HALKETT. 1*s.*

Folio, half-bound boards, India proofs, 21*s*.

## Blake (William).

Etchings from his Works.   By WILLIAM BELL SCOTT.   With descriptive Text.

"*The best side of Blake's work is given here, and makes a really attractive volume, which all can enjoy . . . . The etching is of the best kind, more refined and delicate than the original work.*"—SATURDAY REVIEW.

---

Crown 8vo, cloth extra, gilt, with Illustrations, 7*s*. 6*d*.

## Boccaccio's Decameron;

or, Ten Days' Entertainment.  Translated into English, with an Introduction by THOMAS WRIGHT, Esq., M.A., F.S.A.  With Portrait, and STOTHARD'S beautiful Copperplates.

---

Price One Shilling Monthly, with Four Illustrations.

## Belgravia Magazine.

*That the purpose with which "BELGRAVIA" was originated has been fulfilled, is shown by the popularity that has attended it since its first appearance. Aiming, as may be inferred from its name, at supplying the most refined and cultivated section of London society with intellectual pabulum suited to its requirements, it sprang at once into public favour, and has since remained one of the most extensively read and widely circulated of periodicals. In passing into new hands it has experienced no structural change or modification. Increased energy and increased capital have been employed in elevating it to the highest standard of excellence, but all the features that had won public appreciation have been retained, and the Magazine still seeks its principal support in the homes of Belgravia. As the means through which the writer most readily reaches the heart of the general public, and in consequence as the most important of aids in the establishment of morals and the formation of character, fiction still remains a principal feature in the Magazine. Two Serial Stories accordingly run through its pages; supplemented by short Stories, Novelettes, and narrative or dramatic Sketches: whilst Essays, Social, Biographical, and Humorous; Scientific Discoveries brought to the level of popular comprehension, and treated with a light touch; Poetry, of the highest character; and records of Adventure and Travel, form the remaining portion of the contents. Especial care is now bestowed upon the illustrations, of which no fewer than four appear in each number. Beyond the design of illustrating the article they accompany, these aim at maintaining a position as works of art, both as regards drawing and engraving. In short, whatever claims the Magazine before possessed to favour have now been enhanced, and the Publishers can but leave the result to a public that has seldom failed to appreciate all earnest, persistent, and well-directed efforts for its amusement and benefit.*

\*\* *The THIRTY-FIFTH Volume of BELGRAVIA, elegantly bound in crimson cloth, full gilt side and back, gilt edges, price 7s. 6d., is now ready.—Handsome Cases for binding the volume can be had at 2s. each.*

---

· THIRD EDITION, crown 8vo, cloth extra, gilt, 6*s*.

## Boudoir Ballads:

Vers de Société.  By J. ASHBY-STERRY.

Imperial 4to, cloth extra, gilt and gilt edges, price 21s. per volume.

# Beautiful Pictures by British Artists:

A Gathering of Favourites from our Picture Galleries.  In 2 Series.

The FIRST SERIES including Examples by WILKIE, CONSTABLE, TURNER, MULREADY, LANDSEER, MACLISE, E. M. WARD, FRITH, Sir JOHN GILBERT, LESLIE, ANSDELL, MARCUS STONE, Sir NOEL PATON, FAED, EYRE CROWE, GAVIN O'NEIL, and MADOX BROWN.

The SECOND SERIES containing Pictures by ARMYTAGE, FAED, GOODALL, HEMSLEY, HORSLEY, MARKS, NICHOLLS, Sir NOEL PATON, PICKERSGILL, G. SMITH, MARCUS STONE, SOLOMON, STRAIGHT, E. M. WARD, and WARREN.

All engraved on Steel in the highest style of Art.  Edited, with Notices of the Artists, by SYDNEY ARMYTAGE, M.A.

*" This book is well got up, and good engravings by Jeens, Lumb Stocks, and others, bring back to us pictures of Royal Academy Exhibitions of past years.'* —TIMES.

---

Crown 8vo, with Photographic Portrait, cloth extra, 9s.

# Blanchard's (Laman) Poems.

Now first Collected.  Edited, with a Life of the Author by BLANCHARD JERROLD.

---

Crown 8vo, cloth extra, 7s. 6d.

# Bret Harte's Select Works,

in Prose and Poetry.  With Introductory Essay by J. M. BELLEW, Portrait of the Author, and 50 Illustrations.

*·" Not many months before my friend's death, he had sent me two sketches of a young American writer (Bret Harte), far away in California (' The Outcasts of Poker Flat,' and another), in which he had found such subtle strokes of character as he had not anywhere else in late years discovered ; the manner resembling himself, but the matter fresh to a degree that had surprised him ; the painting in all respects masterly, and the wild rude thing painted a quite wonderful reality.  I have rarely known him more honestly moved."* —FORSTER'S LIFE OF DICKENS

---

Crown 8vo, cloth extra, gilt, 7s. 6d.

# Brand's Observations on Popular Anti-

quities, chiefly Illustrating the Origin of our Vulgar Customs, Ceremonies, and Superstitions.  With the Additions of Sir HENRY ELLIS.  An entirely New and Revised Edition, with fine full-page Illustrations.

---

Small crown 8vo, cloth extra, gilt, with full-page Portraits, 4s. 6d.

# Brewster's (Sir David) Martyrs of

Science.

Small crown 8vo, cloth extra, gilt, with Astronomical Plates, 4s. 6d.

## Brewster's (Sir David) More Worlds

*than One*, the Creed of the Philosopher and the Hope of the Christian.

Small crown 8vo, cloth extra, 6s.

## Brillat-Savarin's Gastronomy as a Fine

*Art;* or, The Science of Good Living. A Translation of the "Physiologie du Goût" of BRILLAT-SAVARIN, with an Introduction and Explanatory Notes by R. E. ANDERSON, M.A.

*"We have read it with rare enjoyment, just as we have delightedly read and re-read quaint old Izaak. Mr. Anderson has done his work of translation daintily, with true appreciation of the points in his original; and altogether, though late, we cannot but believe that this book will be welcomed and much read by many."*—NONCONFORMIST.

Demy 8vo, profusely Illustrated in Colours, price 30s.

## The British Flora Medica:

A History of the Medicinal Plants of Great Britain. Illustrated by a Figure of each Plant, COLOURED BY HAND. By BENJAMIN H. BARTON, F.L.S., and THOMAS CASTLE, M.D., F.R.S. A New Edition, revised, condensed, and partly re-written, by JOHN R. JACKSON, A.L.S., Curator of the Museums of Economic Botany, Royal Gardens, Kew.

THE STOTHARD BUNYAN.—Crown 8vo, cloth extra, gilt, 7s. 6d.

## Bunyan's Pilgrim's Progress.

Edited by Rev. T. SCOTT. With 17 beautiful Steel Plates by STOTHARD, engraved by GOODALL; and numerous Woodcuts.

Crown 8vo, cloth extra, gilt, with Illustrations, 7s. 6d.

## Byron's Letters and Journals.

With Notices of his Life. By THOMAS MOORE. A Reprint of the Original Edition, newly revised, Complete in One thick Volume, with Twelve full-page Plates.

*"We have read this book with the greatest pleasure. Considered merely as a composition, it deserves to be classed among the best specimens of English prose which our age has produced. . . . The style is agreeable, clear, and manly, and when it rises into eloquence, rises without effort or ostentation. It would be difficult to name a book which exhibits more kindness, fairness, and modesty."*—MACAULAY, in the EDINBURGH REVIEW.

Crown 8vo, cloth extra, gilt, 7s. 6d.

## Colman's Humorous Works:

"Broad Grins," "My Nightgown and Slippers," and other Humorous Works, Prose and Poetical, of GEORGE COLMAN. With Life by G. B. BUCKSTONE, and Frontispiece by HOGARTH.

Demy 4to, cloth extra, gilt edges, 31*s*. 6*d*.

# Canova's Works in Sculpture and Model-

*ling.* 150 Plates, exquisitely engraved in Outline by MOSES, and printed on an India tint. With Descriptions by the Countess ALBRIZZI, a Biographical Memoir by CICOGNARA, and Portrait by WORTHINGTON.

"*The fertility of this master's resources is amazing, and the manual labour expended on his works would have worn out many an ordinary workman. The outline engravings are finely executed. The descriptive notes are discriminating, and in the main exact.*"—SPECTATOR.

### NEW VOLUME OF HUNTING SKETCHES.
Oblong 4to, half-bound boards, 21*s*.

# Canters in Crampshire.

By G. BOWERS. I. Gallops from Gorseborough. II. Scrambles with Scratch Packs. III. Studies with Stag Hounds.

"*The fruit of the observation of an artist who has an eye for character, a sense of humour, and a firm and ready hand in delineating characteristic details. . . . . Altogether, this is a very pleasant volume for the tables of country gentlemen, or of those town gentlemen who, like Mr. Black's hero and heroine, divide their time between " Green Pastures and Piccadilly."*—DAILY NEWS.

"*An amusing volume of sketches and adventures in the hunting-field, drawn with great spirit, a keen sense of humour and fun, and no lack of observation.*"—SPECTATOR.

Two Vols. imperial 8vo, cloth extra, gilt, the Plates beautifully printed in Colours, £3 3*s*.

# Catlin's Illustrations of the Manners,

Customs, and Condition of the North American Indians : the result of Eight Years of Travel and Adventure among the Wildest and most Remarkable Tribes now existing. Containing 360 Coloured Engravings from the Author's original Paintings.

Small 4to, cloth gilt, with Coloured Illustrations, 10*s*. 6*d*.

# Chaucer for Children :

A Golden Key. By Mrs. H. R. HAWEIS. With Eight Coloure Pictures and numerous Woodcuts by the Author.

"*It must not only take a high place among the Christmas and New Year books of this season, but is also of permanent value as an introduction to the study of Chaucer, whose works, in selections of some kind or other, are now text-books in every school that aspires to give sound instruction in English.*"—ACADEMY.

Crown 8vo, cloth gilt, Two very thick Volumes, 7*s*. 6*d*. each.

# Cruikshank's Comic Almanack.

Complete in Two SERIES : The FIRST from 1835 to 1843 ; the SECOND from 1844 to 1853. A Gathering of the BEST HUMOUR of THACKERAY, HOOD, MAYHEW, ALBERT SMITH, A'BECKETT, ROBERT BROUGH, &c. With 2000 Woodcuts and Steel Engravings by CRUIKSHANK, HINE, LANDELLS, &c.

Demy 8vo, cloth extra, with Coloured Illustrations and Maps, 24s.

# Cope's History of the Rifle Brigade

(The Prince Consort's Own), formerly the 95th.  By Sir WILLIAM H. COPE, formerly Lieutenant, Rifle Brigade.

" *This latest contribution to the history of the British army is a work of the most varied information regarding the distinguished regiment whose life it narrates, and also of facts interesting to the student in military affairs. . . . Great credit is due to Sir W. Cope for the patience and labour, extending over many years, which he has given to the work. . . . In many cases well-executed plans of actions are given.*"—MORNING POST.

" *Even a bare record of a corps which has so often been under fire, and has borne a part in important engagements all over the world, could not prove otherwise than full of matter acceptable to the military reader.*"—ATHENÆUM.

---

Crown 8vo, cloth extra, gilt, with Portraits, 7s. 6d.

# Creasy's Memoirs of Eminent Etonians;

with Notices of the Early History of Eton College.  By Sir EDWARD CREASY, Author of "The Fifteen Decisive Battles of the World."  A New Edition, brought down to the Present Time, with 13 Illustrations.

" *A new edition of 'Creasy's Etonians' will be welcome.  The book was a favourite a quarter of a century ago, and it has maintained its reputation.  The value of this new edition is enhanced by the fact that Sir Edward Creasy has added to it several memoirs of Etonians who have died since the first edition appeared.  The work is eminently interesting.*"—SCOTSMAN.

---

To be Completed in Twenty-four Parts, quarto, at 5s. each, profusely illustrated by Coloured and Plain Plates and Wood Engravings,

# Cyclopædia of Costume;

or, A Dictionary of Dress—Regal, Ecclesiastical, Civil, and Military—from the Earliest Period in England to the reign of George the Third.  Including Notices of Contemporaneous Fashions on the Continent, and a General History of the Costumes of the Principal Countries of Europe.  By J. R. PLANCHÉ, Somerset Herald.  Part XXI. nearly ready.

" *A most readable and interesting work—and it can scarcely be consulted in vain, whether the reader is in search for information as to military, court, ecclesiastical, legal, or professional costume. . . . All the chromo-lithographs, and most of the woodcut illustrations—the latter amounting to several thousands—are very elaborately executed; and the work forms a livre de luxe which renders it equally suited to the library and the ladies' drawing-room.*"—TIMES.

\*\* The DICTIONARY *forms* Vol. I., *which may now be had bound in half red morocco, price £3 13s. 6d.  Cases for binding 5s. each.*

*The remaining Parts will be occupied by the* GENERAL HISTORY OF THE COSTUMES OF EUROPE, *arranged Chronologically.*

---

Demy 8vo, half-bound morocco, 21s.

# Dibdin's Bibliomania;

or, Book-Madness : A Bibliographical Romance.  With numerous Illustrations.  A New Edition, with a Supplement, including a Key to the Assumed Characters in the Drama.

Parts I. to XII. now ready, 21s. each.

# Cussans' History of Hertfordshire.

By JOHN E. CUSSANS. Illustrated with full-page Plates on Copper and Stone, and a profusion of small Woodcuts.

"*Mr. Cussans has, from sources not accessible to Clutterbuck, made most valuable additions to the manorial history of the county from the earliest period downwards, cleared up many doubtful points, and given original details concerning various subjects untouched or imperfectly treated by that writer. The pedigrees seem to have been constructed with great care, and are a valuable addition to the genealogical history of the county. Mr. Cussans appears to have done his work conscientiously, and to have spared neither time, labour, nor expense to render his volumes worthy of ranking in the highest class of County Histories.'* —ACADEMY.

Demy 8vo, cloth extra, 12s. 6d.

# Doran's Memories of our Great Towns.

With Anecdotic Gleanings concerning their Worthies and their Oddities. By Dr. JOHN DORAN, F.S.A.

"*Lively and conversational; 'brimful,' as the introductory notice in the volume describes them, 'of pleasant chatty interest and antiquarian lore.' . . . The volume will be found useful to ordinary visitors to the towns included within its range. . . . Many of the anecdotes contained in this pleasant collection have not, so far as we know, been published elsewhere.*"—SATURDAY REVIEW.

SECOND EDITION, demy 8vo, cloth gilt, with Illustrations, 18s.

# Dunraven's The Great Divide:

A Narrative of Travels in the Upper Yellowstone in the Summer of 1874. By the EARL of DUNRAVEN. With Maps and numerous striking full-page Illustrations by VALENTINE W. BROMLEY.

"*There has not for a long time appeared a better book of travel than Lord Dunraven's 'The Great Divide.' . . . The book is full of clever observation, and both narrative and illustrations are thoroughly good.*"—ATHENÆUM.

Demy 8vo, cloth extra, with Illustrations, 24s.

# Dodge's (Colonel) The Hunting Grounds

of the Great West : A Description of the Plains, Game, and Indians of the Great North American Desert. By RICHARD IRVING DODGE, Lieutenant-Colonel of the United States Army. With an Introduction by WILLIAM BLACKMORE; Map, and numerous Illustrations drawn by ERNEST GRISET.

"*This magnificent volume is one of the most able and most interesting works which has ever proceeded from an American pen, while its freshness is equal to that of any similar book. Colonel Dodge has chosen a subject of which he is master, and treated it with a fulness that leaves nothing more to be desired, and in a style which is charming equally for its picturesqueness and its purity.*" —NONCONFORMIST.

Crown 8vo, cloth extra, gilt, with Illustrations, 6s.

# Emanuel On Diamonds and Precious

Stones : their History, Value, and Properties ; with Simple Tests for ascertaining their Reality. By HARRY EMANUEL, F.R.G.S. With numerous Illustrations, Tinted and Plain.

Crown 8vo, cloth extra, with Illustrations, 7*s.* 6*d.*

# *The Englishman's House :*

A Practical Guide to all interested in Selecting or Building a House, with full Estimates of Cost, Quantities, &c. By C. J. RICHARDSON. Third Edition. With nearly 600 Illustrations.

\*\*\* *This book is intended to supply a long-felt want, viz., a plain, non-technical account of every style of house, with the cost and manner of building ; it gives every variety, from a workman's cottage to a nobleman's palace.*

---

Crown 8vo, cloth boards, 6*s.* per Volume ; a few Large Paper copies (only 50 printed), at 12*s.* per Vol.

# *Early English Poets.*

Edited, with Introductions and Annotations, by Rev. A. B. GROSART.

*"Mr. Grosart has spent the most laborious and the most enthusiastic care on the perfect restoration and preservation of the text ; and it is very unlikely that any other edition of the poet can ever be called for. . . From Mr. Grosart we always expect and always receive the final results of most patient and competent scholarship."*—EXAMINER.

1. *Fletcher's (Giles, B.D.) Complete Poems :* Christ's Victorie in Heaven, Christ's Victorie on Earth, Christ's Triumph over Death, and Minor Poems. With Memorial-Introduction and Notes. One Vol.

2. *Davies' (Sir John) Complete Poetical Works,* including Psalms I. to L. in Verse, and other hitherto Unpublished MSS., for the first time Collected and Edited. With Memorial-Introduction and Notes. Two Vols.

3. *Herrick's (Robert) Hesperides, Noble Numbers, and* Complete Collected Poems. With Memorial-Introduction and Notes, Steel Portrait, Index of First Lines, and Glossarial Index, &c. Three Vols.

4. *Sidney's (Sir Philip) Complete Poetical Works,* including all those in "Arcadia." With Portrait, Memorial-Introduction, Essay on the Poetry of Sidney, and Notes. Three Vols.

5. *Donne's (Dr. John) Complete Poetical Works,* including the Satires and various from MSS. With Memorial-Introduction and Notes.

[*In preparation.*

---

*IMPORTANT VOLUME OF ETCHINGS.*

Folio, cloth extra, £1 11*s.* 6*d.*

# *Examples of Contemporary Art.*

Etchings from Representative Works by living English and Foreign Artists. Edited, with Critical Notes, by J. COMYNS CARR.

*"It would not be easy to meet with a more sumptuous, and at the same time a more tasteful and instructive drawing-room book."*—NONCONFORMIST.

Crown 8vo, cloth extra, with Illustrations, 6s.

## Fairholt's Tobacco:

Its History and Associations; with an Account of the Plant and its Manufacture, and its Modes of Use in all Ages and Countries. By F. W. FAIRHOLT, F.S.A. A New Edition, with Coloured Frontispiece and upwards of 100 Illustrations by the Author.

"*A very pleasant and instructive history of tobacco and its associations, which we cordially recommend alike to the votaries and to the enemies of the muck-maligned but certainly not neglected weed. . . . Full of interest and information.*"—DAILY NEWS.

Crown 8vo, cloth extra, with Illustrations, 7s. 6d.

## Finger-Ring Lore:

Historical, Legendary, and Anecdotal.—Earliest Notices; Superstitions; Ring Investiture, Secular and Ecclesiastical; Betrothal and Wedding Rings; Ring-tokens; Memorial and Mortuary Rings; Posy-Rings; Customs and Incidents in Connection with Rings; Remarkable Rings, &c. By WILLIAM JONES, F.S.A. With Hundreds of Illustrations of Curious Rings of all Ages and Countries.

"*Enters fully into the whole subject, and gives an amount of information and general reading in reference thereto which is of very high interest. The book is not only a sort of history of finger-rings, but is a collection of anecdotes in connection with them. . . . The volume is admirably illustrated, and altogether affords an amount of amusement and information which is not otherwise easily accessible.*"—SCOTSMAN.

"*One of those gossiping books which are as full of amusement as of instruction.*"—ATHENÆUM.

THE RUSKIN GRIMM.—Square crown 8vo, cloth extra, 6s. 6d.; gilt edges, 7s. 6d.

## German Popular Stories.

Collected by the Brothers GRIMM, and Translated by EDGAR TAYLOR. Edited, with an Introduction, by JOHN RUSKIN. With 22 Illustrations after the inimitable designs of GEORGE CRUIKSHANK. Both Series Complete.

"*The illustrations of this volume . . . . are of quite sterling and admirable art, of a class precisely parallel in elevation to the character of the tales which they illustrate; and the original etchings, as I have before said in the Appendix to my 'Elements of Drawing,' were unrivalled in masterfulness of touch since Rembrandt (in some qualities of delineation, unrivalled even by him). . . . To make somewhat enlarged copies of them, looking at them through a magnifying glass, and never putting two lines where Cruikshank has put only one, would be an exercise in decision and severe drawing which would leave afterwards little to be learnt in schools.*"—Extract from Introduction by JOHN RUSKIN.

One Vol. crown 8vo, cloth extra, 9s.

## Gilbert's (W. S.) Original Plays:

"A Wicked World," "Charity," "The Palace of Truth," "Pygmalion," "Trial by Jury," &c.

"*His workmanship is in its way perfect; it is very sound, very even, very well sustained, and excellently balanced throughout.*"—OBSERVER.

Crown 8vo, cloth extra, with Illustrations, 4s. 6d.

## Faraday's Chemical History of a Candle.

Lectures delivered to a Juvenile Audience.   A New Edition.
Edited by W. CROOKES, F.C.S.   With numerous Illustrations.

Crown 8vo, cloth extra, with Illustrations, 4s. 6d.

## Faraday's Various Forces of Nature.

A New Edition.   Edited by W. CROOKES, F.C.S.   With numerous
Illustrations.

One Shilling Monthly, Illustrated by ARTHUR HOPKINS.

## The Gentleman's Magazine.

Edited by SYLVANUS URBAN, Gentleman.

*In seeking to restore the "GENTLEMAN'S MAGAZINE" to the position
it formerly held, the Publishers do not lose sight of the changed conditions
under which it now appears.  While maintaining an historical continuity which
dates back to the reign of George the Second, there will be no attempt to burden
the present with the weight of a distant past, or to adhere slavishly to traditions
the application of which is unsuited to the altered conditions of society at the
present time.   It is sought to render the Magazine to the gentleman of to-day
what in earlier times it proved to the gentleman of a past generation.   New
features will be introduced to take the place of those which disappear; in the
most important respects, however, the connecting links between the present and
the past will be closest.   Biography and History, which have always formed a
conspicuous portion of the contents, will retain the prominence assigned them,
and will be treated with the added breadth that springs from increased familiarity with authorities and more exact appreciation of the province of the
Biographer and the Historian.   Science, which confers upon the age special
eminence, will have its latest conclusions and forecasts presented in a manner
which shall bring them within the grasp of the general reader.   The philosophical aspect of Politics, the matters which affect Imperial interests, will be
separated from the rivalries of party, and will receive a due share of attention.
Archæology (under which comprehensive head may be included Genealogy, To-
pography, and other similar matters), Natural History, Sport and Adventure,
Poetry, Belles Lettres, Art in all its manifestations, will constitute a portion
of the contents; and Essays upon social subjects will, as heretofore, be interspersed.   Under the head of Table Talk matters of current interest will be
discussed, and facts of historic value will be preserved.   A Work of Fiction by
some novelist of highest position will run through the pages of the Magazine,
and will be illustrated by artists of known excellence.   With a full sense of
what is involved in their promise, and with a firm resolution to abide by their
pledges, the Publishers undertake to spare no exertion that is necessary to secure
the highest class of contributions, to place the Magazine in the first rank of
serials, and to fit it to take its place on the table and on the shelves of all classes
of cultivated Englishmen.*

\*\* *Now ready, the Volume for* JANUARY *to* JUNE, 1878, *cloth extra,
price* 8s. 6d. ; *and Cases for binding, price* 2s. *each.*

Demy 4to, cloth extra, with Illustrations, 31s. 6d.

## Gillray the Caricaturist:

The Story of his Life and Times, with Anecdotal Descriptions of
his Engravings.   Edited by THOMAS WRIGHT, Esq., M.A., F.S.A.
With 83 full-page Plates, and numerous Wood Engravings.

Crown 8vo, cloth gilt and gilt edges, 7s. 6d.

# The Golden Treasury of Thought :

AN ENCYCLOPÆDIA OF QUOTATIONS from Writers of all Times and Countries.  Selected and Edited by THEODORE TAYLOR.

Square 16mo (Tauchnitz size), cloth extra, 2s. per volume

# The Golden Library :

**Bayard Taylor's Diver-**sions of the Echo Club.

**The Book of Clerical Anec-**dotes.

**Byron's Don Juan.**

**Carlyle (Thomas) on the** Choice of Books.  With a Memoir.  1s. 6d.

**Emerson"'s Letters and** Social Aims.

**Godwin's (William) Lives** of the Necromancers.

**Holmes's Autocrat of the** Breakfast Table.  With an Introduction by G. A. SALA.

**Holmes's Professor at the** Breakfast Table.

**Hood's Whims and Oddi-**ties.  Complete.  With all the original Illustrations.

**Irving's  (Washington)** Tales of a Traveller.

**Irving's  (Washington)** Tales of the Alhambra.

**Jesse's (Edward) Scenes** and Occupations of Country Life.

**Lamb's Essays of Elia.** Both Series Complete in One Vol.

**Leigh Hunt's Essays : A** Tale for a Chimney Corner, and other Pieces.  With Portrait, and Introduction by EDMUND OLLIER

**Mallory's (Sir Thomas)** Mort d'Arthur : The Stories of King Arthur and of the Knights of the Round Table.  Edited by B. MONTGOMERIE RANKING.

**Pascal's Provincial Let-**ters.  A New Translation, with Historical Introduction and Notes, by T. M'CRIE, D.D., LL.D.

**Pope's Complete Poetical** Works.

**Rochefoucauld's Maxims** and Moral Reflections.  With Notes, and an Introductory Essay by SAINTE-BEUVE.

**St. Pierre's Paul and** Virginia, and the Indian Cottage.  Edited, with Life, by the Rev. E. CLARKE.

**Shelley's  Early  Poems** and Queen Mab, with Essay by LEIGH HUNT.

**Shelley's Later Poems :** Laon and Cythna, &c.

**Shelley's Posthumous** Poems, the Shelley Papers, &c.

**Shelley's Prose Works,** including A Refutation of Deism, Zastrozzi, St. Irvyne, &c.

**White's Natural History** of Selborne.  Edited, with additions, by THOMAS BROWN, F.L.S.

*" A series of excellently printed and carefully annotated volumes, handy in size, and altogether attractive."*—BOOKSELLER.

Small 8vo, cloth gilt, 6s.

## Gosse's King Erik :

A Tragedy. By EDMUND W. GOSSE. Vignette by W. B. SCOTT.
" *We have seldom seen so marked an advance in a second book beyond a first. Its merits are solid and of a very high order.*"—ACADEMY.

Small 8vo, cloth gilt, 5s.

## Gosse's On Viol and Flute.

Second Edition. With a Vignette by W. B. SCOTT.

Half-bound, paper boards, 21s.; or elegantly half-bound crimson morocco, gilt, 25s.

## The Graphic Portfolio.

Fifty Engravings from "The Graphic," most carefully printed on the finest plate paper (18 in. by 15 in.) from the Original Engravings. The Drawings are by S. L. FILDES, HELEN PATERSON, HUBERT HERKOMER, SYDNEY HALL, E. J. GREGORY, G. D. LESLIE, W. SMALL, G. DU MAURIER, Sir JOHN GILBERT, G. J. PINWELL, CHARLES GREEN, G. DURAND, M. E. EDWARDS, A. B. HOUGHTON, H. S. MARKS, F. W. LAWSON, H. WEIGALL, and others.

"*Contains some of the choicest specimens, both of drawing and wood-engraving. Admirable in details and expression, and engraved with rare delicacy.*"—DAILY NEWS.

Demy 8vo, cloth extra, with Illustrations, 21s.

## Greeks and Romans (The Life of the),

Described from Antique monuments. By ERNST GUHL and W. KONER. Translated from the Third German Edition, and Edited by Dr. F. HUEFFER. With 545 Illustrations.

Crown 8vo, cloth extra, gilt, with Illustrations, 7s. 6d.

## Greenwood's Low-Life Deeps :

An Account of the Strange Fish to be found there ; including "The Man and Dog Fight," with much additional and confirmatory evidence ; "With a Tally-Man," "A Fallen Star," "The Betting Barber," "A Coal Marriage," &c. By JAMES GREENWOOD. With Illustrations in tint by ALFRED CONCANEN.

Crown 8vo, cloth extra, gilt, with Illustrations, 4s. 6d.

## Guyot's Earth and Man ;

or, Physical Geography in its Relation to the History of Mankind. With Additions by Professors AGASSIZ, PIERCE, and GRAY. 12 Maps and Engravings on Steel, some Coloured, and a copious Index.

Crown 8vo, cloth extra, gilt, with Illustrations, 7s. 6d.

## Greenwood's Wilds of London:

Descriptive Sketches, from Personal Observations and Experience, of Remarkable Scenes, People, and Places in London. By JAMES GREENWOOD. With 12 Tinted Illustrations by ALFRED CONCANEN.

"*Mr. James Greenwood presents himself once more in the character of ' one whose delight it is to do his humble endeavour towards exposing and extirpating social abuses and those hole-and-corner evils which afflict society.'*"—SATURDAY REVIEW.

Large 4to, price ONE GUINEA, with 14 facsimile plates.

## The Grosvenor Gallery Illustrated Catalogue

*logue* — Winter Exhibition (1877–78) of Drawings by the Old Masters and Water-Colour Drawings by Deceased Artists of the British School. With a Critical Introduction by J. COMYNS CARR.

"*Turning to Mr. COMYNS CARR's essay on the drawings of the Italian Masters, we may say that it is undeniably the most finished piece of critical writing that has fallen from his hand.*"—ACADEMY.

"*Mr. COMYNS CARR's Illustrated Catalogue of the Grosvenor Gallery Exhibition of Drawings last year, with his admirable introduction and careful photographic illustrations. It costs a guinea, and is worth a great deal more. Exquisite alike in its text and its illustrations.*"—PUNCH.

Crown 8vo, cloth extra, 6s.

## Hake's New Symbols:

Poems. By THOMAS GORDON HAKE.

"*The entire book breathes a pure and ennobling influence, shows welcome originality of idea and illustration, and yields the highest proof of imaginative faculty and mature power of expression.*"—ATHENÆUM.

Medium 8vo, cloth extra, gilt, with Illustrations, 7s. 6d.

## Hall's (Mrs. S. C.) Sketches of Irish

*Character.* With numerous Illustrations on Steel and Wood by DANIEL MACLISE, Sir JOHN GILBERT, W. HARVEY, and G. CRUIKSHANK.

"*The Irish Sketches of this lady resemble Miss Mitford's beautiful English Sketches in ' Our Village,' but they are far more vigorous and picturesque and bright.*"—BLACKWOOD'S MAGAZINE.

Small 8vo, cloth limp, with Illustrations, 2s. 6d.

## The House of Life;

HUMAN PHYSIOLOGY, with its Applications to the Preservation of Health. For use in Classes, and Popular Reading. With numerous Illustrations. By Mrs. F. FENWICK MILLER.

Three Vols. royal 4to, cloth boards, £6 6s.

## Historical Portraits ;

Upwards of 430 Engravings of Rare Prints. Comprising the Collections of RODD, RICHARDSON, CAULFIELD, &c. With Descriptive Text to every Plate, giving a brief outline of the most important Historical and Biographical Facts and Dates connected with each Portrait, and references to original Authorities.

Two Vols. royal 8vo, with Coloured Frontispieces, cloth extra, £2 5s.

## Hope's Costume of the Ancients.

Illustrated in upwards of 320 Outline Engravings, containing Representations of Egyptian, Greek, and Roman Habits and Dresses.

*" The substance of many expensive works, containing all that may be necessary to give to artists, and even to dramatic performers and to others engaged in classical representations, an idea of ancient costumes sufficiently ample to prevent their offending in their performances by gross and obvious blunders.*

Crown 8vo, cloth extra, gilt, 7s. 6d.

## Hood's (Thomas) Choice Works,

In Prose and Verse. Including the CREAM OF THE COMIC ANNUALS. With Life of the Author, Portrait, and over Two Hundred original Illustrations.

*" Not only does the volume include the better-known poems by the author, but also what is happily described as ' the Cream of the Comic Annuals.' Such delicious things as ' Don't you smell Fire?' ' The Parish Revolution,' and ' Huggins and Duggins, will never want readers."*—GRAPHIC.

Crown 8vo, cloth extra, with Photographic Portrait, 6s.

## Hood's (Tom) Poems, Humorous and

*Pathetic.* Edited, with a Memoir, by his Sister, FRANCES FREELING BRODERIP.

*" There are many poems in the volume which the very best judge might well mistake for his father's work."*—STANDARD.

Square crown 8vo, in a handsome and specially-designed binding, gilt edges, 6s.

## Hood's (Tom) From Nowhere to the

*North Pole:* A Noah's Arkæological Narrative. With 25 Illustrations by W. BRUNTON and E. C. BARNES.

*" The amusing letterpress is profusely interspersed with the jingling rhymes which children love and learn so easily. Messrs. Brunton and Barnes do full justice to the writer's meaning, and a pleasanter result of the harmonious co-operation of author and artist could not be desired."*—TIMES.

Crown 8vo, cloth extra, gilt, 7s. 6d.

# Hook's (Theodore) Choice Humorous

**Works,** including his Ludicrous Adventures, Bons-mots, Puns, and Hoaxes. With a new Life of the Author, Portraits, Fac-similes, and Illustrations.

Demy 8vo, cloth extra, 12s. 6d.

# Hueffer's The Troubadours:

A History of Provençal Life and Literature in the Middle Ages. By FRANCIS HUEFFER.

" *This attractive volume deals in a very fresh and exact way with a most interesting phase of culture and letters. . . . . Mr. Hueffer claims for his volume the praise of being the first adequate study on so famous a subject as the Troubadours which has appeared in the English language; and we believe that we must allow that he is right. His book will be found exceedingly interesting and valuable. . . . . It is a grateful task to review a volume where so firm a ground of scholarship is under our feet, and where there is so little need to be on the watch for instances of inaccuracy or want of knowledge. . . . Mr. Hueffer is to be congratulated on a very important contribution to literature.*"—EXAMINER.

Crown 8vo, cloth extra, 7s. 6d.

# Howell's The Conflicts of Capital and

**Labour,** Historically and Economically considered. Being a History and Review of the Trade Unions of Great Britain, showing their Origin, Progress, Constitution, and Objects, in their Political, Social, Economical, and Industrial Aspects. By GEORGE HOWELL.

" *A complete account of trades unions, involving the most candid statement of their objects and aspirations, their virtues and faults, is of great value; and such Mr. Howell's book will be found by those who consult it. . . . Far from being the impassioned utterance of an advocate, it is, on the contrary, a calm, authoritative statement of facts, and the expression of the views of the workmen and their leaders. . . . The book is a storehouse of facts, some of them extremely well arranged. . . . . His book is of profound interest. We have no hesitation in giving it our hearty praise.*"—ECHO.
" *This book is an attempt, and on the whole a successful attempt, to place the work of trade unions in the past, and their objects in the future, fairly before the public from the working man's point of view.*"—PALL MALL GAZETTE.

Atlas folio, half morocco, gilt, £5 5s.

# The Italian Masters:

Autotype Facsimiles of Original Drawings in the British Museum. With Critical and Descriptive Notes, Biographical and Artistic, by J. COMYNS CARR.

" *This splendid volume. . . Mr. Carr's choice of examples has been dictated by wide knowledge and fine tact. . . The majority have been reproduced with remarkable accuracy. Of the criticism which accompanies the drawings we have not hitherto spoken, but it is this which gives the book its special value.*"—PALL MALL GAZETTE.

Crown 8vo, cloth extra, 7s.

## *Horne's Orion:*

An Epic Poem, in Three Books. By RICHARD HENGIST HORNE.
Tenth Edition.

" *Orion will be admitted, by every man of genius, to be one of the noblest, if not the very noblest, poetical work of the age. Its defects are trivial and conventional, its beauties intrinsic and supreme.*"—EDGAR ALLAN POE.

Small 8vo, cloth extra, 6s.

## *Jeux d'Esprit,*

Written and Spoken, of the Later Wits and Humourists. Collected
and Edited by HENRY S. LEIGH.

" *This thoroughly congenial piece of work* . . . *Mr. Leigh's claim to praise is threefold: he has performed the duty of taster with care and judgment; he has restored many stolen or strayed bons-mots to their rightful owners; and he has exercised his editorial functions delicately and sparingly.*"—DAILY TELEGRAPH.

Two Vols. 8vo, with 52 Illustrations and Maps, cloth extra, gilt, 14s.

## *Josephus's Complete Works.*

Translated by WHISTON. Containing both "The Antiquities of
the Jews," and "The Wars of the Jews."

Small 8vo, cloth, full gilt, gilt edges, with Illustrations, 6s.

## *Kavanaghs' Pearl Fountain,*

And other Fairy Stories. By BRIDGET and JULIA KAVANAGH.
With Thirty Illustrations by J. MOYR SMITH.

" *Genuine new fairy stories of the old type, some of them as delightful as the best of Grimm's 'German Popular Stories.'* . . . . *For the most part, the stories are downright, thorough-going fairy stories of the most admirable kind.* . . . . *Mr. Moyr Smith's illustrations, too, are admirable. Look at that white rabbit. Anyone would see at the first glance that he is a rabbit with a mind, and a very uncommon mind too—that he is a fairy rabbit, and that he is posing as chief adviser to some one—without reading even a word of the story. Again, notice the fairy-like effect of the little picture of the fairy-bird ' Don't-forget-me,' flying away back into fairy-land. A more perfectly dream-like impression of fairy-land has hardly been given in any illustration of fairy tales within our knowledge.*"—SPECTATOR.

Small 8vo, cloth extra, 5s.

## *Lamb's Poetry for Children, and Prince*

*Dorus.* Carefully reprinted from unique copies.

" *The quaint and delightful little book, over the recovery of which all the hearts of his lovers are yet warm with rejoicing.*"—Mr. SWINBURNE, in the ATHENÆUM.

Crown 8vo, cloth, full gilt, 6s. (uniform with "Boudoir Ballads.")

## *Leigh's A Town Garland.*

By HENRY S. LEIGH, Author of "Carols of Cockayne."

Crown 8vo, cloth extra, gilt, with Portraits, 7*s.* 6*d.*

# Lamb's Complete Works,

In Prose and Verse, reprinted from the Original Editions, with many Pieces hitherto unpublished. Edited, with Notes and Introduction, by R. H. SHEPHERD. With Two Portraits and Facsimile of a page of the "Essay on Roast Pig."

"*A complete edition of Lamb's writings, in prose and verse, has long been wanted, and is now supplied. The editor appears to have taken great pains to bring together Lamb's scattered contributions, and his collection contains a number of pieces which are now reproduced for the first time since their original appearance in various old periodicals.*"—SATURDAY REVIEW.

---

Crown 8vo, cloth extra, with numerous Illustrations, 10*s.* 6*d.*

# Mary & Charles Lamb:

Their Poems, Letters, and Remains. With Reminiscences and Notes by W. CAREW HAZLITT. With HANCOCK's Portrait of the Essayist, Facsimiles of the Title-pages of the rare First Editions of Lamb's and Coleridge's Works, and numerous Illustrations.

"*Very many passages will delight those fond of literary trifles; hardly any portion will fail in interest for lovers of Charles Lamb and his sister.*"—STANDARD.

---

Demy 8vo, cloth extra, with Maps and Illustrations, 18*s.*

# Lamont's Yachting in the Arctic Seas;

or, Notes of Five Voyages of Sport and Discovery in the Neighbourhood of Spitzbergen and Novaya Zemlya. By JAMES LAMONT, F.R.G.S. With numerous full-page Illustrations by Dr. LIVESAY.

"*After wading through numberless volumes of icy fiction, concocted narrative, and spurious biography of Arctic voyagers, it is pleasant to meet with a real and genuine volume. . . He shows much tact in recounting his adventures, and they are so interspersed with anecdotes and information as to make them anything but wearisome. . . . The book, as a whole, is the most important addition made to our Arctic literature for a long time.*"—ATHENÆUM.

---

Crown 8vo, cloth, full gilt, 7*s.* 6*d.*

# Latter-Day Lyrics:

Poems of Sentiment and Reflection by Living Writers; selected and arranged, with Notes, by W. DAVENPORT ADAMS. With a Note on some Foreign Forms of Verse, by AUSTIN DOBSON.

"*A useful and eminently attractive book.*"—ATHENÆUM.

"*One of the most attractive drawing-room volumes we have seen for a long time.*"—NONCONFORMIST.

"*The volume is one that should find a place on the bookshelf of every cultivated man or woman. The lyrics are chosen with rare taste and perspicacity. Mr. Davenport Adams undoubtedly possesses the artistic art of selection.*"—LIVERPOOL COURIER.

Crown 8vo, cloth extra, 8s. 6d.

## Lee's More Glimpses of the World Unseen.

Edited by the Rev. FREDERICK GEORGE LEE, D.C.L., Vicar of All Saints', Lambeth; Editor of "The Other World; or, Glimpses of the Supernatural," &c.

In preparation, crown 8vo, cloth extra, illustrated, 10s. 6d.

## Leisure-Time Studies.

By Dr. ANDREW WILSON, F.R.P.S., &c., Lecturer on Zoology and Comparative Anatomy, Edinburgh School of Medicine; Examiner in Medicine, University of Glasgow, &c.

*The Volume will contain Chapters on the following among other subjects—Biology and its Teachings—Science and Education—A Study of Lower Life—Moot Points in Biology—Sea Serpents – Some Facts and Fictions of Zoology—Animal Architects—The Law of Likeness—The Distribution of Animals—The Origin of Nerves—Animal Development and what it Teaches—Animals and their Environments, &c. &c.*

Crown 8vo, cloth extra, with Illustrations, 7s. 6d.

## Life in London;

or, The History of Jerry Hawthorn and Corinthian Tom. With the whole of CRUIKSHANK'S Illustrations, in Colours, after the Originals.

Crown 8vo, cloth extra, with Illustrations, 7s. 6d.

## Longfellow's Complete Prose Works.

Including "Outre Mer," "Hyperion," "Kavanagh," "The Poets and Poetry of Europe," and "Driftwood." With Portrait and Illustrations by VALENTINE BROMLEY.

Crown 8vo, cloth extra, gilt, with Illustrations, 7s. 6d.

## Longfellow's Poetical Works.

Carefully Reprinted from the Original Editions. With numerous fine Illustrations on Steel and Wood.

*" Mr. Longfellow has for many years been the best known and the most read of American poets; and his popularity is of the right kind, and rightly and fairly won. He has not stooped to catch attention by artifice, nor striven to force it by violence. His works have faced the test of parody and burlesque (which in these days is almost the common lot of writings of any mark), and have come off unharmed."*—SATURDAY REVIEW.

Second Edition, crown 8vo, cloth extra, 5s.

## MacColl's Three Years of the Eastern

Question. By the Rev. MALCOLM MACCOLL, M.A.

*" I hope I shall not seem obtrusive in expressing to you the pleasure with which I have read your " Three Years of the Eastern Question." The tide is running so hard against the better cause just now that one feels specially impelled to offer one's thanks to those who stand firm, particularly when they state our case so admirably as you have."*—GOLDWIN SMITH.

Small crown 8vo, cloth extra, 4s. 6d.

# Linton's Joshua Davidson,

Christian and Communist. By E. LYNN LINTON. Sixth Edition, with a New Preface.

THE FRASER PORTRAITS.—Demy 4to, cloth gilt and gilt edges, with 83 characteristic Portraits, 31s. 6d.

# Maclise's Gallery of Illustrious Literary

*Characters.* With Notes by Dr. MAGINN. Edited, with copious Additional Notes, by WILLIAM BATES, B.A.

"*One of the most interesting volumes of this year's literature.*"—TIMES.

" *Deserves a place on every drawing-room table, and may not unfitly be removed from the drawing-room to the library.*"—SPECTATOR.

Crown 8vo, cloth extra, with Illustrations, 2s. 6d.

# Madre Natura v. The Moloch of Fashion.

By LUKE LIMNER. With 32 Illustrations by the Author. FOURTH EDITION, revised and enlarged.

" *Agreeably written and amusingly illustrated. Common sense and erudition are brought to bear on the subjects discussed in it.*"—LANCET.

Crown 8vo, cloth extra, 6s.

# Lights on the Way:

Some Tales within a Tale. By the late J. H. ALEXANDER, B.A. Edited, with an Explanatory Note, by H. A. PAGE, Author of "Thoreau : a Study."

Handsomely printed in facsimile, price 5s.

# Magna Charta.

An exact Facsimile of the Original Document in the British Museum, printed on fine plate paper, nearly 3 feet long by 2 feet wide, with the Arms and Seals of the Barons emblazoned in Gold and Colours.

\*\*\* A full Translation, with Notes, on a large sheet, 6d.

Crown 8vo, cloth extra, 7s. 6d.

# Maid of Norway (The).

Translated from the German by Mrs. BIRKBECK. With Pen and Ink Sketches of Norwegian Scenery.

Small 8vo, cloth extra, with Illustrations, 7s. 6d.

# Mark Twain's Adventures of Tom Sawyer.

With One Hundred Illustrations.

" *A book to be read. There is a certain freshness and novelty about it, a practically romantic character, so to speak, which will make it very attractive.*"—SPECTATOR.

\*\*\* Also a Popular Edition, post 8vo, illustrated boards, 2s.

*NEW COPYRIGHT WORK BY MARK TWAIN.*
Post 8vo, illustrated boards, 2s.

# An Idle Excursion, and other Papers.
By MARK TWAIN.

Crown 8vo, cloth extra, with Illustrations, 7s. 6d.

# Mark Twain's Choice Works.
Revised and Corrected throughout by the Author. With Life, Portrait, and numerous Illustrations.

Post 8vo, illustrated boards, 2s.

# Mark Twain's Pleasure Trip on the
Continent of Europe. ("The Innocents Abroad," and "The New Pilgrim's Progress.")

Two Vols. crown 8vo, cloth extra, 18s.

# Marston's (Dr. Westland) Dramatic
and Poetical Works. Collected Library Edition.
"The 'Patrician's Daughter' is an oasis in the desert of modern dramatic literature, a real emanation of mind. We do not recollect any modern work in which states of thought are so freely developed, except the 'Torquato Tasso' of Goethe. The play is a work of art in the same sense that a play of Sophocles is a work of art; it is one simple idea in a state of gradual development . . . 'The Favourite of Fortune' is one of the most important additions to the stock of English prose comedy that has been made during the present century."—TIMES.

Crown 8vo, cloth extra, 8s.

# Marston's (Philip B.) All in All:
Poems and Sonnets.

Handsomely half-bound, India Proofs, royal folio, £10 ; Large Paper copies, Artists' India Proofs, elephant folio, £20.

# Modern Art:
A Series of superb Line Engravings, from the Works of Distinguished Painters of the English and Foreign Schools, selected from Galleries and Private Collections in Great Britain. With descriptive Text by JAMES DAFFORNE.

Crown 8vo, cloth extra, gilt, gilt edges, 7s. 6d.

# Muses of Mayfair:
Vers de Société of the Nineteenth Century. Including Selections from TENNYSON, BROWNING, SWINBURNE, ROSSETTI, JEAN INGELOW, LOCKER, INGOLDSBY, HOOD, LYTTON, C. S. C.; LANDOR, AUSTIN DOBSON, &c. Edited by H. C. PENNELL.

Crown 8vo, cloth extra, 8s.

# Marston's (Philip B.) Song Tide,

And other Poems.   Second Edition.

Crown 8vo, cloth extra, 6s.

# The New Republic;

or, Culture, Faith, and Philosophy in an English Country House.
By W. H. MALLOCK.

*" The great charm of the book lies in the clever and artistic way the dialogue is managed, and the diverse and various expedients by which, whilst the love of thought on every page is kept at a high pitch, it never loses its realistic aspect. . . . It is giving high praise to a work of this sort to say that it absolutely needs to be taken as a whole, and that disjointed extracts here and there would entirely fail to convey any idea of the artistic unity, the careful and conscientious sequence of what is evidently the brilliant outcome of much patient thought and study. . . . Enough has now been said to recommend these volumes to any reader who desires something above the usual novel, something which will open up lanes of thought in his own mind, and insensibly introduce a higher standard into his daily life. . . . Here is novelty indeed, as well as originality, and to anyone who can appreciate or understand 'The New Republic,' it cannot fail to be a rare treat."*—OBSERVER.

Square 8vo, cloth extra, with numerous Illustrations, 9s.

# North Italian Folk.

By Mrs. COMYNS CARR.   With Illustrations by RANDOLPH CALDECOTT.

*" A delightful book, of a kind which is far too rare.   If anyone wants to really know the North Italian folk, we can honestly advise him to omit the journey, and sit down to read Mrs. Carr's pages instead. . . . Description with Mrs. Carr is a real gift . . . It is rarely that a book is so happily illustrated."*—CONTEMPORARY REVIEW.

*MOORE'S HITHERTO UNCOLLECTED WRITINGS.*
Crown 8vo, cloth extra, with Frontispiece, 9s.

# Prose and Verse—Humorous, Satirical,

and Sentimental—by *THOMAS MOORE.*   Including Suppressed Passages from the Memoirs of Lord Byron.   Chiefly from the Author's MSS., and all hitherto Inedited and Uncollected.   Edited, with Notes, by RICHARD HERNE SHEPHERD.

*" Hitherto Thomas Moore has been mostly regarded as one of the lighter writers merely—a sentimental poet par excellence, in whom the 'rapture of love and of wine' determined him strictly to certain modes of sympathy and of utterance, and these to a large extent of a slightly artificial character.   This volume will serve to show him in other, and certainly as attractive, aspects, while, at the same time, enabling us to a considerable extent to see how faithfully he developed himself on the poetical or fanciful side. . . . This is a book which claims, as it ought to obtain, various classes of readers, and we trust that the very mixed elements of interest in it may not conflict with its obtaining them.   For the lightest reader there is much to enjoy; for the most thoughtful something to ponder over; and the thanks of both are due to editor and publisher alike."*—NONCONFORMIST.

*NEW WORK by the Author of " THE NEW REPUBLIC."*
Crown 8vo, cloth extra, 3s. 6d.

## The New Paul and Virginia;

or, Positivism on an Island.   By W. H. MALLOCK, Author of "The New Republic."

Crown 8vo, cloth extra, with Vignette Portraits, price 6s. per Vol.

## The Old Dramatists:

### Ben Jonson's Works.

With Notes, Critical and Explanatory, and a Biographical Memoir by WILLIAM GIFFORD. Edited by Col. CUNNINGHAM. Three Vols.

### Chapman's Works.

Now First Collected.   Complete in Three Vols.   Vol. I. contains the Plays complete, including the doubtful ones ;   Vol. II. the Poems and Minor Translations, with an Introductory Essay by

ALGERNON CHARLES SWINBURNE ; Vol. III. the Translations of the Iliad and Odyssey.

### Marlowe's Works.

Including his Translations. Edited, with Notes and Introduction, by Col. CUNNINGHAM. One Vol.

### Massinger's Plays.

From the Text of WILLIAM GIFFORD. With the addition of the Tragedy of "Believe as you List." Edited by Col. CUNNINGHAM. One Vol.

Fcap. 8vo, cloth extra, 6s.

## O'Shaughnessy's (Arthur) An Epic of

*Women*, and other Poems.   Second Edition.

Crown 8vo, cloth extra, 10s. 6d.

## O'Shaughnessy's Lays of France.

(Founded on the "Lays of Marie.")   Second Edition.

Fcap. 8vo, cloth extra, 7s. 6d.

## O'Shaughnessy's Music and Moonlight:

Poems and Songs.

Crown 8vo, illustrated boards, with numerous Plates, 2s. 6d.

## Old Point Lace, and How to Copy and

*Imitate It.*   By DAISY WATERHOUSE HAWKINS.   With 17 Illustrations by the Author.

Crown 8vo, carefully printed on creamy paper, and tastefully bound in cloth for the Library, price 6s. each.

## The Piccadilly Novels:

### Popular Stories by the Best Authors.

Antonina.                                    By WILKIE COLLINS.
Illustrated by Sir J. GILBERT and ALFRED CONCANEN.

Basil.                                       By WILKIE COLLINS.
Illustrated by Sir JOHN GILBERT and J. MAHONEY.

## The Piccadilly Novels—*continued.*

### *Patricia Kemball.*
By E. Lynn Linton.

With Frontispiece by G. Du Maurier.

" *Displays genuine humour, as well as keen social observation. Enough graphic portraiture and witty observation to furnish materials for half-a-dozen novels of the ordinary kind.*"—Saturday Review.

### *The Atonement of Leam Dundas.*
By E. Lynn Linton.

With a Frontispiece by Henry Woods.

" *In her narrowness and her depth, in her boundless loyalty, her self-forgetting passion, that exclusiveness of love which is akin to cruelty, and the fierce humility which is vicarious pride, Leam Dundas is a striking figure. In one quality the authoress has in some measure surpassed herself.*"—Pall Mall Gaz.

### *The Waterdale Neighbours.*
By Justin McCarthy.

### *My Enemy's Daughter.*
By Justin McCarthy.

### *Linley Rochford.*
By Justin McCarthy.

### *A Fair Saxon.*
By Justin McCarthy.

### *Dear Lady Disdain.*
By Justin McCarthy.

### *The Evil Eye, and other Stories.*
By Katharine S. Macquoid.

Illustrated by Thomas R. Macquoid and Percy Macquoid.

"*Cameos delicately, if not very minutely or vividly, wrought, and quite finished enough to give a pleasurable sense of artistic ease and faculty. A word of commendation is merited by the illustrations.*"—Academy.

### *Number Seventeen.*
By Henry Kingsley.

### *Oakshott Castle.*
By Henry Kingsley.

With a Frontispiece by Shirley Hodson.

"*A brisk and clear north wind of sentiment—sentiment that braces instead of enervating—blows through all his works, and makes all their readers at once healthier and more glad.*"—Spectator.

### *Open! Sesame!*
By Florence Marryat.

Illustrated by F. A. Fraser.

" *A story which arouses and sustains the reader's interest to a higher degree than, perhaps, any of its author's former works.*"—Graphic.

### *Whiteladies.*
By Mrs. Oliphant.

With Illustrations by A. Hopkins and H. Woods.

" *A pleasant and readable book, written with practical ease and grace.*"—Times.

### *The Best of Husbands.*
By James Payn.

Illustrated by J. Moyr Smith.

### *Fallen Fortunes.*
By James Payn.

### *Halves.*
By James Payn.

With a Frontispiece by J. Mahoney.

### *Walter's Word.*
By James Payn.

Illustrated by J. Moyr Smith.

### *What he Cost her.*
By James Payn.

" *His novels are always commendable in the sense of art. They also possess another distinct claim to our liking : the girls in them are remarkably charming and true to nature, as most people, we believe, have the good fortune to observe nature represented by girls.*"—Spectator.

## THE PICCADILLY NOVELS—*continued.*

*Her Mother's Darling.*   By Mrs. J. H. RIDDELL

*The Way we Live Now.*   By ANTHONY TROLLOPE.
With Illustrations.

*The American Senator.*   By ANTHONY TROLLOPE.

"*Mr. Trollope has a true artist's idea of tone, of colour, of harmony: his pictures are one, and seldom out of drawing; he never strains after effect, is fidelity itself in expressing English life, is never guilty of caricature."—*
FORTNIGHTLY REVIEW.

*Diamond Cut Diamond.*   By T. A. TROLLOPE.

"*Full of life, of interest, of close observation, and sympathy. . . . When Mr. Trollope paints a scene it is sure to be a scene worth painting."—*SATUR-
DAY REVIEW.

*Bound to the Wheel.*   By JOHN SAUNDERS.

*Guy Waterman.*   By JOHN SAUNDERS.

*One Against the World.*   By JOHN SAUNDERS.

*The Lion in the Path.*   By JOHN SAUNDERS.

"*A carefully written and beautiful story—a story of goodness and truth, which is yet as interesting as though it dealt with the opposite qualities. . . . The author of this really clever story has been at great pains to work out all its details with elaborate conscientiousness, and the result is a very vivid picture of the ways of life and habits of thought of a hundred and fifty years ago. . . . Certainly a very interesting book."—*TIMES.

*Ready-Money Mortiboy.*   By W. BESANT and JAMES RICE.

*My Little Girl.*   By W. BESANT and JAMES RICE.

*The Case of Mr. Lucraft.*   By W. BESANT and JAMES RICE.

*This Son of Vulcan.*   By W. BESANT and JAMES RICE.

*With Harp and Crown.*   By W. BESANT and JAMES RICE.

*The Golden Butterfly.*   By W. BESANT and JAMES RICE.
With a Frontispiece by F. S. WALKER.

"'*The Golden Butterfly' will certainly add to the happiness of mankind, for . defy anybody to read it with a gloomy countenance."—*TIMES.

---

*NEW NOVEL BY JUSTIN MᶜCARTHY.*

Two vols. 8vo, cloth extra, Illustrated, 21*s*., the THIRD EDITION of

## Miss Misanthrope.

By JUSTIN MCCARTHY, Author of "Dear Lady Disdain," &c.
With 12 Illustrations by ARTHUR HOPKINS.

"*In 'Miss Misanthrope' Mr. McCarthy has added a new and delightful portrait to his gallery of Englishwomen. . . . It is a novel which may be sipped like choice wine; it is one to linger over and ponder; to be enjoyed like fine, sweet air, or good company, for it is pervaded by a perfume of honesty and humour, of high feeling, of kindly penetrating humour, of good sense, and wide knowledge of the world, of a mind richly cultivated and amply stored. There is scarcely a page in these volumes in which we do not find some fine remark or felicitous reflection of piercing, yet gentle and indulgent irony."—*DAILY NEWS.

## *MRS. LINTON'S NEW NOVEL.*

Two Vols. 8vo, cloth extra, Illustrated, 21*s*., the SECOND EDITION of

# *The World Well Lost.*

By E. LYNN LINTON, Author of "Patricia Kemball," &c. With 12 Illustrations by HENRY FRENCH and J. LAWSON.

*"If Mrs. Linton had not already won a place among our foremost living novelists, she would have been entitled to it by her latest work of fiction—a book of singularly high and varied merit. The story rivets the attention of the reader at the outset, and holds him absorbed until the close."*—SCOTSMAN.

## *MR. JAMES PAYN'S NEW NOVEL.*

Two Vols., 8vo, cloth extra, Illustrated, 21*s*., the SECOND EDITION of

# *By Proxy.*

By JAMES PAYN, Author of "Walter's Word," &c. With 12 Illustrations by ARTHUR HOPKINS.

*"One of the most racy and entertaining of English novels."*—ILLUSTRATED LONDON NEWS.

## *NEW NOVEL BY MR. JAMES GRANT.*
### Three Vols., crown 8vo.

# *The Lord Hermitage.*

By JAMES GRANT, Author of "The Romance of War," &c.

## *OUIDA'S NEW NOVEL.*
### Now ready, in Three Vols., crown 8vo.

# *Friendship :*

A Story of Society. By OUIDA.

### Crown 8vo, red cloth, extra, 5*s*. each.

# *Ouida's Novels.—Uniform Edition.*

| | | | |
|---|---|---|---|
| *Held in Bondage.* By OUIDA. | *Puck.* | By OUIDA. |
| *Strathmore.* By OUIDA. | *Folle Farine.* | By OUIDA. |
| *Chandos.* By OUIDA. | *Dog of Flanders.* | By OUIDA. |
| *Under Two Flags.* By OUIDA. | *Pascarel.* | By OUIDA. |
| *Idalia.* By OUIDA. | *Two Wooden Shoes* By OUIDA. |
| *Tricotrin.* By OUIDA. | *Signa.* | By OUIDA. |
| *Cecil Castlemaine's Gage.* By OUIDA. | *In a Winter City.* By OUIDA. |
| | *Ariadnê.* | By OUIDA. |

### Small 8vo, cloth extra, with Illustrations, 3*s*. 6*d*.

# *The Prince of Argolis :*

A Story of the Old Greek Fairy Time. By J. MOYR SMITH. With 130 Illustrations by the Author.

Post 8vo, illustrated boards, 2s. each.

# Cheap Editions of Popular Novels.

[WILKIE COLLINS' NOVELS may also be had in cloth limp at 2s. 6d. See, too, the PICCADILLY NOVELS, for Library Editions.]

*The Woman in White.*          By WILKIE COLLINS.

*Antonina.*          By WILKIE COLLINS.

*Basil.*          By WILKIE COLLINS.

*Hide and Seek.*          By WILKIE COLLINS.

*The Dead Secret.*          By WILKIE COLLINS.

*The Queen of Hearts.*          By WILKIE COLLINS.

*My Miscellanies.*          By WILKIE COLLINS.

*The Moonstone.*          By WILKIE COLLINS.

*Man and Wife.*          By WILKIE COLLINS.

*Poor Miss Finch.*          By WILKIE COLLINS.

*Miss or Mrs.?*          By WILKIE COLLINS.

*The New Magdalen.*          By WILKIE COLLINS.

*The Frozen Deep.*          By WILKIE COLLINS.

*The Law and the Lady.*          By WILKIE COLLINS.

*Gaslight and Daylight.*          By GEORGE AUGUSTUS SALA.

*The Waterdale Neighbours.*          By JUSTIN MCCARTHY.

*My Enemy's Daughter.*          By JUSTIN MCCARTHY.

*Linley Rochford.*          By JUSTIN MCCARTHY.

*A Fair Saxon.*          By JUSTIN MCCARTHY.

*Dear Lady Disdain.*          By JUSTIN MCCARTHY.

*An Idle Excursion.*          By MARK TWAIN.

*The Adventures of Tom Sawyer.*          By MARK TWAIN.

*Pleasure Trip on the Continent of Europe.*          MARK TWAIN.

*Oakshott Castle.*          By HENRY KINGSLEY.

*Bound to the Wheel.*          By JOHN SAUNDERS.

*Guy Waterman.*          By JOHN SAUNDERS.

*One Against the World.*          By JOHN SAUNDERS.

*The Lion in the Path.*          By JOHN and KATHERINE SAUNDERS.

*Surly Tim.*          By the Author of "That Lass o' Lowrie s."

*Under the Greenwood Tree.*          By THOMAS HARDY.

*Ready-Money Mortiboy.*          By WALTER BESANT and JAMES RICE.

*The Golden Butterfly.*          By Authors of "Ready-Money Mortiboy."

*This Son of Vulcan.*          By the Authors of "Ready-Money Mortiboy."

*My Little Girl.*          By the Authors of "Ready-Money Mortiboy."

*The Case of Mr. Lucraft.*          Authors of "Ready-Money Mortiboy."

*With Harp and Crown.*          Authors of "Ready-Money Mortiboy."

Two Vols. 8vo, cloth extra, with Illustrations, 10s. 6d.

# Plutarch's Lives of Illustrious Men.

Translated from the Greek, with Notes Critical and Historical, and a Life of Plutarch, by JOHN and WILLIAM LANGHORNE. New Edition, with Medallion Portraits.

Crown 8vo, cloth extra, with Portrait and Illustrations, 7s. 6d.

# Poe's Choice Prose and Poetical Works.

With BAUDELAIRE'S "Essay."

*" Poe stands as much alone among verse-writers as Salvator Rosa among painters."*—SPECTATOR.

Crown 8vo, cloth extra, Illustrated, 7s. 6d.

# The Life of Edgar Allan Poe.

By WILLIAM F. GILL. With numerous Illustrations and Facsimiles.

Demy 8vo, cloth extra, 12s. 6d.

# Proctor's Myths and Marvels of Astronomy.

By RICHARD A. PROCTOR, Author of "Other Worlds than Ours," &c.

*" Mr. Proctor, who is well and widely known for his faculty of popularising the latest results of the science of which he is a master, has brought together in these fascinating chapters a curious collection of popular beliefs concerning divination by the stars, the influences of the moon, the destination of the comets, the constellation figures, and the habitation of other worlds than ours."*—DAILY NEWS.

Crown 8vo, cloth extra, 5s.

# Prometheus the Fire-Giver :

An attempted Restoration of the Lost First Part of the Trilogy of Æschylus.

*" Another illustration of that classical revival which is due in no small degree to the influence of Mr. Swinburne. . . . Much really fine writing, and much appreciation of the Æschylean spirit."*—HOME NEWS.

*" Well written in parts—soft, spirited, and vigorous, according to requirement."*
—ILLUSTRATED LONDON NEWS.

In Two Series, small 4to, blue and gold, gilt edges, 6s. each.

# Puniana ;

or, Thoughts Wise and Other-Why's. A New Collection of Riddles, Conundrums, Jokes, Sells, &c. In Two Series, each containing 3000 of the best Riddles, 10,000 most outrageous Puns, and upwards of Fifty beautifully executed Drawings by the Editor, the Hon. HUGH ROWLEY. Each Series is Complete in itself.

*" A witty, droll, and most amusing work, profusely and elegantly illustrated."*
—STANDARD.

Crown 8vo, cloth extra, with Portrait and Facsimile, 12s. 6d.

# The Final Reliques of Father Prout.

Collected and Edited, from MSS. supplied by the family of the Rev. FRANCIS MAHONY, by BLANCHARD JERROLD.

Crown 8vo, cloth extra, gilt, 7s. 6d.

# The Pursuivant of Arms ;

or, Heraldry founded upon Facts. A Popular Guide to the Science of Heraldry. By J. R. PLANCHÉ, Esq., Somerset Herald. With Coloured Frontispiece, Plates, and 200 Illustrations.

Crown 8vo, cloth extra, 7s. 6d.

# Rabelais' Works.

Faithfully Translated from the French, with variorum Notes, and numerous Characteristic Illustrations by GUSTAVE DORÉ.

Crown 8vo, cloth gilt, with numerous Illustrations, and a beautifully executed Chart of the various Spectra, 7s. 6d., a New Edition of

# Rambosson's Astronomy.

By J. RAMBOSSON, Laureate of the Institute of France. Translated by C. B. PITMAN. Profusely Illustrated.

Crown 8vo, cloth extra, 6s.

# Red-Spinner's By Stream and Sea :

A Book for Wanderers and Anglers. By WILLIAM SENIOR (RED-SPINNER).

"*Mr. Senior has long been known as an interesting and original essayist. He is a keen observer, a confessed lover of ' the gentle sport,' and combines with a fine picturesque touch a quaint and efficient humour. All these qualities come out in a most attractive manner in this delightful volume. . . . It is pre-eminently a bright and breezy book, full of nature and odd out-of-the-way references. . . We can conceive of no better book for the holiday tour or the seaside.*"—NONCONFORMIST.

"*Very delightful reading; just the sort of book which an angler or a rambler will be glad to have in the side pocket of his jacket. Altogether, ' By Stream and Sea ' is one of the best books of its kind which we have come across for many a long day.*"—OXFORD UNIVERSITY HERALD.

Crown 8vo, cloth extra, 7s. 6d.

# Memoirs of the Sanson Family :

Seven Generations of Executioners. By HENRI SANSON. Translated from the French, with Introduction, by CAMILLE BARRÈRE.

"*A faithful translation of this curious work, which will certainly repay perusal —not on the ground of its being full of horrors, for the original author seems to be rather ashamed of the technical aspect of his profession, and is commendably reticent as to its details, but because it contains a lucid account of the most notable causes célèbres from the time of Louis XIV. to a period within the memory of persons still living. . . . Can scarcely fail to be extremely entertaining.*"— DAILY TELEGRAPH.

In reduced facsimile, small 8vo, half Roxburghe, 10s. 6d.

# The First Folio Shakespeare.

Mr. WILLIAM SHAKESPEARE'S Comedies, Histories, and Tragedies. Published according to the true Originall Copies. London,
Printed by ISAAC IAGGARD and ED. BLOUNT, 1623.—An exact
Reproduction of the extremely rare original, in reduced facsimile
by a photographic process—ensuring the strictest accuracy in every
detail. *A full Prospectus will be sent upon application.*

*" To Messrs. Chatto and Windus belongs the merit of having done more to
facilitate the critical study of the text of our great dramatist than all the Shakespeare clubs and societies put together. A complete facsimile of the celebrated
First Folio edition of 1623 for half-a-guinea is at once a miracle of cheapness and
enterprise. Being in a reduced form, the type is necessarily rather diminutive,
but it is as distinct as in a genuine copy of the original, and will be found to be as
useful and far more handy to the student than the latter."—*ATHENÆUM.

---

Two Vols. crown 8vo, cloth extra, 18s.

# The School of Shakspere.

Including "The Life and Death of Captain Thomas Stukeley,"
with a New Life of Stucley, from Unpublished Sources; "No-
body and Somebody," "Histriomastix," "The Prodigal Son,"
"Jack Drum's Entertainement," "A Warning for Fair Women,'
with Reprints of the Accounts of the Murder; and "Faire Em.'
Edited, with Introductions and Notes, and an Account of Robert
Green and his Quarrels with Shakspere, by RICHARD SIMPSON,
B.A., Author of "The Philosophy of Shakspere's Sonnets," "The
Life of Campion," &c. With an Introduction by F. J. FURNIVALL.

---

Crown 8vo, cloth extra, with Illustrations, 7s. 6d.

# Signboards :

Their History. With Anecdotes of Famous Taverns and Remarkable Characters. By JACOB LARWOOD and JOHN CAMDEN
HOTTEN. With nearly 100 Illustrations.

*" Even if we were ever so maliciously inclined, we could not pick out all Messrs.
Larwood and Hotten's plums, because the good things are so numerous as to defy
the most wholesale depredation."—*TIMES.

---

Crown 8vo, cloth extra, gilt, 6s. 6d.

# The Slang Dictionary :

Etymological, Historical, and Anecdotal. An ENTIRELY NEW
EDITION, revised throughout, and considerably Enlarged.

*" We are glad to see the Slang Dictionary reprinted and enlarged. From a high
scientific point of view this book is not to be despised. Of course it cannot fail to
be amusing also. It contains the very vocabulary of unrestrained humour, and
oddity, and grotesqueness. In a word, it provides valuable material both for the
student of language and the student of human nature."—*ACADEMY.

Exquisitely printed in miniature, cloth extra, gilt edges, 2s. 6d.

## The Smoker's Text-Book.

By J. HAMER, F.R.S.L.

Crown 8vo, cloth extra, gilt, with 10 full-page Tinted
Illustrations, 7s. 6d.

## Sheridan's Complete Works,

with Life and Anecdotes. Including his Dramatic Writings,
printed from the Original Editions, his Works in Prose and
Poetry, Translations, Speeches, Jokes, Puns, &c.; with a Collection of Sheridaniana.

"*The editor has brought together within a manageable compass not only the
seven plays by which Sheridan is best known, but a collection also of his poetical
pieces which are less familiar to the public, sketches of unfinished dramas, selections
from his reported witticisms, and extracts from his principal speeches. To these
is prefixed a short but well-written memoir, giving the chief facts in Sheridan's
literary and political career; so that, with this volume in his hand, the student
may consider himself tolerably well furnished with all that is necessary for a
general comprehension of the subject of it.*"— PALL MALL GAZETTE.

Crown 4to, uniform with "Chaucer for Children," with Coloured
Illustrations, cloth gilt, 10s. 6d.

## Spenser for Children.

By M. H. TOWRY. With Illustrations in Colours by WALTER
J. MORGAN.

"*Spenser has simply been transferred into plain prose, with here and there a
line or stanza quoted, where the meaning and the diction are within a child's
comprehension, and additional point is thus given to the narrative without the
cost of obscurity. . . . Altogether the work has been well and carefully done.*"
—THE TIMES.

Imperial 4to, containing 150 beautifully-finished full-page Engravings
and Nine Vignettes, all tinted, and some illuminated in gold and
colours, half-morocco, £9 9s.

## Stothard's Monumental Effigies of Great

*Britain.* With Historical Description and Introduction by JOHN
KEMPE, F.S.A. A NEW EDITION, with a large body of Additional
Notes by JOHN HEWITT.

\*\*\* A few Large Paper copies, royal folio, with the arms illuminated
in gold and colours, and the plates very carefully finished in body-colours,
heightened with gold in the very finest style, half-morocco, £15 15s.

Crown 8vo, cloth extra, 9s.

## Stedman's Victorian Poets:

Critical Essays. By EDMUND CLARENCE STEDMAN.

"*We ought to be thankful to those who do critical work with competent skill
and understanding, with honesty of purpose, and with diligence and thoroughness
of execution. And Mr. Stedman, having chosen to work in this line, deserves the
thanks of English scholars by these qualities and by something more; . . . .
he is faithful, studious, and discerning.*"—SATURDAY REVIEW.

# Mr. Swinburne's Works :

### The Queen Mother and
Rosamond. Fcap. 8vo, 5s.

### Atalanta in Calydon.
A New Edition. Crown 8vo, 6s.

### Chastelard.
A Tragedy. Crown 8vo, 7s.

### Poems and Ballads.
Fcap. 8vo, 9s. Also in crown 8vo, at same price.

### Notes on "Poems and
Ballads." 8vo, 1s.

### William Blake :
A Critical Essay. With Facsimile Paintings. Demy 8vo, 16s.

### Songs before Sunrise.
Crown 8vo, 10s. 6d.

### Bothwell :
A Tragedy. Two Vols. crown 8vo, 12s. 6d.

### George Chapman :
An Essay. Crown 8vo, 7s.

### Songs of Two Nations.
Crown 8vo, 6s.

### Essays and Studies.
Crown 8vo, 12s.

### Erechtheus :
A Tragedy. Crown 8vo, 6s.

### Note of an English Re-
publican on the Muscovite Crusade. 8vo, 1s.

### A Note on Charlotte Brontë.
Crown 8vo, 6s.

---

MR. SWINBURNE'S NEW WORK.
Crown 8vo, cloth extra, 9s.

# Poems and Ballads. SECOND SERIES.
By ALGERNON CHARLES SWINBURNE.

\*\*\* Also in fcap. 8vo, at same price, uniform with the FIRST SERIES.

---

Fcap. 8vo, cloth extra, 3s. 6d.

# Rossetti's (W. M.) Criticism upon Swin-
burne's " Poems and Ballads."

---

Crown 8vo, cloth extra, with Illustrations, 7s. 6d.

# Swift's Choice Works,
in Prose and Verse. With Memoir, Portrait, and Facsimiles of the Maps in the Original Edition of "Gulliver's Travels."

" *The 'Tale of a Tub' is, in my apprehension, the masterpiece of Swift; certainly Rabelais has nothing superior, even in invention, nor anything so condensed, so pointed, so full of real meaning, of biting satire, of felicitous analogy. The 'Battle of the Books' is such an improvement on the similar combat in the Lutrin, that we can hardly own it as an imitation.*"—HALLAM.

" *If he had never written either the 'Tale of a Tub' or 'Gulliver's Travels,' his name merely as a poet would have come down to us, and have gone down to posterity, with well-earned honours.*"—HAZLITT.

Crown 8vo, cloth extra, with Illustrations, 7s. 6d.

## Strutt's Sports and Pastimes of the

People of England; including the Rural and Domestic Recreations, May Games, Mummeries, Shows, Processions, Pageants, and Pompous Spectacles, from the Earliest Period to the Present Time. With 140 Illustrations. Edited by WILLIAM HONE.

*.* A few Large Paper Copies, with an extra set of Copperplate Illustrations, carefully Coloured by Hand, from the Originals, 50s.

---

Medium 8vo, cloth extra, with Illustrations, 7s. 6d.

## Dr. Syntax's Three Tours,

in Search of the Picturesque, in Search of Consolation, and in Search of a Wife. With the whole of ROWLANDSON's droll page Illustrations, in Colours, and Life of the Author by J. C. HOTTEN.

---

Large post 8vo, cloth, full gilt, gilt top, with Illustrations, 12s. 6d.

## Thackerayana:

Notes and Anecdotes Illustrated by a profusion of Sketches by WILLIAM MAKEPEACE THACKERAY, depicting Humorous Incidents in his School-life, and Favourite Characters in the books of his everyday reading. With Hundreds of Wood Engravings and Five Coloured Plates, from Mr. Thackeray's Original Drawings.

*"It would have been a real loss to bibliographical literature had copyright difficulties deprived the general public of this very amusing collection. One of Thackeray's habits, from his schoolboy days, was to ornament the margins and blank pages of the books he had in use with caricature illustrations of their contents. This gave special value to the sale of his library, and is almost cause for regret that it could not have been preserved in its integrity. Thackeray's place in literature is eminent enough to have made this an interest to future generations. The anonymous editor has done the best that he could to compensate for the lack of this. It is an admirable addendum, not only to his collected works, but also to any memoir of him that has been, or that is likely to be, written."—BRITISH QUARTERLY REVIEW.*

---

Crown 8vo, cloth extra, gilt edges, with Illustrations, 7s. 6d.

## Thomson's Seasons and Castle of Indolence.

With a Biographical and Critical Introduction by ALLAN CUNNINGHAM, and over 50 fine Illustrations on Steel and Wood.

---

Crown 8vo, cloth extra, with Coloured Illustrations, 7s. 6d.

## J. M. W. Turner's Life and Correspondence.

Founded upon Letters and Papers furnished by his Friends and fellow Academicians. By WALTER THORNBURY. A New Edition, considerably Enlarged. With numerous Illustrations in Colours, facsimiled from Turner's original Drawings.